I0538261

Aberrant Literature Short Fiction Collection

Volume I

Edited by

Jason Peters

www.AberrantLiterature.com

@AberrantLit

Hello from Aberrant Literature,

Thanks so much for checking out this collection of some of the most inventive and creative short fiction you're likely to come across. At Aberrant Literature, our goal is for you to have a unique experience via the power of creative fiction. It is our belief that in a literary landscape populated by recycled and tired ideas, there are many unique and wonderful voices looking for an audience, and it is our aim to bring them to you. It is our sincere hope that you will appreciate the level of ingenuity on display, and will join us on our journey as we search the country for the best and most creative short fiction on the horizon.

Stay Aberrant,

Jason Peters

Editor-In-Chief

Table of Contents

A Trial By Any Other Name

by Jason Peters

The crowd filled the stadium near completion; several different beings from several different galaxies, all congregated in the giant arena that stood proud in its strength and worn elegance. For one day out of every four years by way of the Human measurement of time, beings from all across the universe send their best, brightest, and wealthiest to attend and participate in the Galactic Olympiad, respectfully referencing the historic tournaments of Earth by the same name.

Walls standing several stories tall surrounded an empty pit of dry dirt, which was to serve as the centerpiece for the day's action. Row upon row of bleachers were filled to capacity, with a number of those in attendance proudly waving banners and flags representing the colors of their galaxy, along with the crests of their most influential and respected families. On either side of the pit stood large pathways that would serve as a holding ground for the participants, with opponents held from each other's view prior to the proceedings, so as to ensure that any action took place strictly on the battlefield. It was customary for royalty to be given the right side, a not-so-subtle statement, while slaves, often referred to as "battle chum," were to be held on the left.

Within the slave grounds to the left, a new batch of Recruits trudged by way of chains into the pen. A typical group of Recruits was comprised of refugees and political defectors, though several prisoners-of-war had become victims of the trafficking industry as well. As with any group of living property, there was a wrangler, and his name was Skeeter.

A being of average height and above-average intellect for a Human, Skeeter, named as such on account of, "He's always buzzing in and out of places quicker than you can catch him," walked alongside the new Recruits as they gathered in the pen, heads held low and feet shuffling through the dirt. As the last of the eight Recruits trudged into the pen, Skeeter closed the swinging gate and latched it shut, proceeding to take inventory. By the man's account, he had one Acriot, three Humans, two Second Plutonians, one Cartrellion, and one vicious-looking Arachneophyte. Skeeter knew he had to be careful around the Arachneophyte, as they were well-known for their erratic and violent temperament. What's worse is that few families ever elected to have their representative do battle with them, as most were afraid of the consequences to what were almost exclusively a given family's best warriors, meaning Skeeter had to be on guard for the duration of the ceremony.

Having catalogued the Recruits, he then turned to address them.

"Listen up. You all know why you're here. Now obviously, this isn't where you expected to find yourself in life. You got dealt a terrible hand; there's no denying that. However, with that being said, it's not necessarily a given that today has to be the day of your death. For starters, there are eight of you and only six contestants, which means that at least two of you will live to see another day. Secondly, if any of you are warriors, trained through instruction or experience, you've done battle before. 'This isn't your first rodeo,' as the popular expression on my planet goes. It will be a tough battle, but a battle one and the same; one with a yet-to-be-determined outcome. Not to mention that for those of you skilled in weaponry, there will be several…"

"We're starving," one of the humans, a woman, interrupted. "How do we stand a chance when we're too weak to barely even walk?" Skeeter had not the heart to tell them this was done by design. However, he had consistently made a point ever since the first games to smuggle in food for the Recruits. It was a barbaric enough act to force captives into the games as it were; to starve them for several days leading up to the Olympiad to serve up an easier victory for the visiting families of significance seemed to go against the fairness of competition. "I have food for you," announced Skeeter, causing all of the creatures faces to light up, save for the Arachneophyte, who possessed a complex digestive system that only necessitated eating a substantial portion of food once a week. "I will return; do not try to escape. I promise you will find certain and resolute death if you try to escape. You are now an investment; purchased property upon which your investor hopes to yield a substantial profit. Investors do not take their loss of assets lightly."

Skeeter turned around and headed down the corridor to retrieve the hidden food. As he turned a corner and was no longer in sight, nearly all of the slaves attempted to free themselves of the chains attached to their neck, arms, and ankles, with exception to the Human woman, and the Arachneophyte, who looked as though he could not be bothered with petty trifles such as food. One by one, the Recruits gave up in their attempts as they realized the futility of their efforts. As the last one of them, a human male, continued to wrestle with the chains, he began to look unwell. His face, in addition to any other visible skin, became increasingly white. The man began to tremble and convulse, causing the rest of the recruits to keep their distance as much as the chains would allow. The convulsions became more violent and he began foaming at the mouth, and it seemed as though he might spontaneously combust at any moment. Then, at the moment of critical mass, the human instantly morphed into a small six-legged creature that resembled a goat as interpreted by an alien race. The Recruits all jumped in place and scattered as much as physically possible as the six-legged goat creature bleated an unrecognizable honking sound, and began running in the opposite direction towards the pit. As he continued out of the corridor into the middle of the pit, the onlookers all pointed and gasped at the peculiar sight of a small six-legged creature scampering across the pit with all his might. He ran considerably fast, and was roughly two thirds of the way across the field barreling towards the opposing holding ground entrance, when suddenly, there was a sharp, high-pitched squeal as the creature stopped dead in his tracks and fell to the ground dead, his body motionless as its overly long tongue hung outside of its mouth.

The members of the audience collectively gasped, then fell silent for several moments. A young being from the Orcanick Nebula seated in the front row allowed his curiosity to get the better of him, and leaped out from his seat and onto the battlefield. As he walked on all four appendages over to the dead body of the creature, the crowd erupted into cheers once more. Upon reaching the body, the being searched the area around the corpse, whereupon he found a baseball-sized stone covered in the purple blood that the being could now see leaking and pooling from the side of the goat's head. He picked it up and held it to the sky, turning the stone as he observed it. To the audience, it looked as though the being was displaying it for all to see, though this did not cross the young beings mind as he looked out onto the horizon from the direction of where the rock most certainly came from. He squinted his eyes and zoomed his vision towards the horizon, where in the distance he could see the small spec of a figure. It looked to be brown, though he couldn't be certain from his vantage point.

As the young being looked out towards the advancing figure in the distance, a small troupe of roughly two dozen men came marching out of the corridor to the right, all regaled in a multitude of colors representing the many different cultures, kingdoms, planets, and families represented at the Galactic Olympiad. They stopped in the center of the pit and raised a series of brass instruments, some recognizable as creations of Earth, others significant contributions from other members of the universe. In unison, the two dozen musicians blared their instruments in a long, drawn out rhythm. As the notes continued to play, an Acriot, a blue-skinned creature resembling a Human in shape and form, though possessing a system of intricate reproductive organs that allow them to spawn asexually under certain temporal and geographic conditions, marched out onto the grounds of the pit. She matched a yellow outfit resembling a sundress with a bright green shawl wrapped around the top of her head.

Back in the left corridor, Skeeter turned the corner back towards the slaves and dropped the cheese and smoked meat as he immediately noticed one of the Recruits missing.

"Where'd he go?" Skeeter demanded.

"The man," the Human woman declared, "he turned into a small six-legged goat and ran off into the battlefield. There was quite a commotion. I can't be certain of what occurred."

Skeeter looked over the rest of the Recruits. "Is that true?" he asked of them. The slaves all subtly and reluctantly shook their heads in agreement, ashamed of their attempts at escape, or at least feigning as much in hopes that Skeeter would show the mercy and still provide them their meal. Skeeter bent down to pick the food up off of the ground. "The Shapeshifter is dead," he declared as he picked up the last of the cheese and meat and extended the food to the starving creatures that eagerly consumed every last morsel given to them. "I suppose that only guarantees one of you left alive, now," Skeeter remarked.

Out in the pit, the blue scales of the Acriot glimmered in the light and heat cast by the third star of the planet Gorash, casting small, jittery reflections upon the spectators. As she spoke, her voice carried throughout the arena thanks to carefully placed noise amplifiers, calibrated so as to respond only to the specific frequency emitted by her voice.

"To the many beings of the universe that have gathered here today," she commenced, "I welcome you on behalf of the Committee of the Galactic Olympiad."

There was a large, sustained applause from the audience.

"I am Ambassador Elocusia," she continued, "representative of the planet Troma 17, and speaker of the Montarian people. We assemble before the many Gods of the Universe today in celebration of the creation of being; the very essence of life that courses through all of us, bringing us together in spite of our differences, and reminding us that our limits are determined only by our imagination, or lack thereof. Many of you are friends, whilst others remain enemies. Yet, in a profound display of respect, we have collectively chosen to ignore past and current hostilities in celebration of the awe-inspiring light of being. You humble yourselves before the Gods, as do I. May the strength and virility of life be with you always."

As was tradition, the collective beings in attendance bowed their head in a moment of silence. This went on for several moments until a slight rumbling began to make its presence known. It came in brief, sudden waves, each progressively louder and more intense than the previous. Certain of the beings in the stands with more advanced eyesight than others began to point at the horizon, causing others to follow suit. As the being on the horizon more fully came into view, there was enormous enthusiasm, and slowly the crowd begin to cheer until the being, and his thunderous footsteps, came to a stop in full and complete view.

"My Fellow Beings of Creation, join me in welcoming our esteemed referee of today's events, The Overseer!"

"All Glory to The Overseer!" announced the spectators unanimously, followed by more enthusiastic applause. The Overseer stood proud and tall, a being fashioned entirely out of out of stone and rock that assimilated its incredible mass over time, as small fragments of intergalactic rock and dust would attach themselves to him when attracted by The Overseer's life energy, and ever-increasing gravitational pull. After several centuries of roaming the galaxy as the only being of his kind, his considerable mass stood nearly the height of the walls of the arena.

Back in the left corridor, the slaves were cowering, covered in dust and soot that had been shaken loose from the walls by way of the force exerted from The Overseer's gargantuan steps.

"Are we going to die now?" asked a shaken Second Plutonian.

"Probably not," explained Skeeter. "That's just The Overseer. As long as you don't try to escape, you need only worry about death at the hands of your combatant."

"Comforting," responded the other Second Plutonian, who was faring a bit better than his counterpart, but not by much.

From the middle of the battle pit, Ambassador Elocusia announced the words that officially kicked off every Galactic Olympiad. "Now, as they say on Earth, let the games begin!"

The crowd responded accordingly, and a loud and thunderous applause echoed throughout the stadium, and across the barren desert of Apprichondia, where this year's games were held. "Please welcome the first Esteemed Representative, Sir Vorn Trindesaad, Duke of Ambergrenst, and son to Othedran. The Duke strode out confidently, dressed head to toe in a luminescent robe that seemed to embody all colors at once. Upon reaching the center of the pit, he rose one of several hands high in the air, and graciously bowed to the audience, once again causing a chorus of cheers to erupt. Ambassador Elocusia looked to the two guards at her left, and gave a subtle nod. They returned her signal, and turned around, clanging their large battle axes against one another's three separate and distinct times.

Skeeter looked back at the guards, understanding that the time had come for the games to take place. He took one more glance at the indentured combatants and sighed as he swung the arm of the pen open. "It's time," he said as he grabbed hold of the chains and led the group towards their destiny, which lay in wait in the middle of the battlefield.

With the guards standing to attention at either side of the entrance to the pit, Skeeter marched the Recruits out into the sunlight, the lot of them greeted by immense applause. As he looked back, he could see all of the creatures' heads down, with exception to the Human woman. She was staring intently into Skeeter's eyes, her head held high with a stern, unafraid expression. Skeeter returned her hard gaze. This was not common behavior for a Recruit almost certainly staring down her last days.

"I wonder what she's trying to tell me," Skeeter thought.

His thinking was interrupted when the Arachneophyte begin to buck against Skeeter's lead. The creature's strength was impressive, and Skeeter began to feel him losing grip of the chains. However, one strong and sudden motion from The Overseer, staring down at the Arachneophyte with a disapproving gaze, was all it took to subdue the violent creature by way of intimidation.

Skeeter and the rest of the Recruits continued until they reached the middle of the arena, the crowd slowly lowering the applause until it had all but dissipated. Sir Trindesaad walked over to the seven lowly-looking slaves and inspected them up and down as they stood with their heads lowered. After walking back and forth, looking them over several times, the being took a deliberate step backwards and stood stiffly and at attention. With a slow, deliberate raise of his hand, he pointed towards one of the two Second Plutonians. The crowd erupted in approval. The Duke then looked to his right, signaling his guards, who turned and knocked their battle axes against each other three times, as was the custom, before retrieving a large rack from the corridor and carrying it out to the pit. The rack contained several weapons, from Earthen constructs such as a crossbow and a battle axe similar to the one's wielded by the guards, to far more elaborate selections from other worlds. The Second Plutonian was then asked to select from the available options, eventually settling on a large broadsword that elicited chuckles from several of the spectators, as few assumed the Second Plutonian would be able to handle such an enormous weapon.

Moments later, the crowd collectively gasped as the chosen warrior emerged from the right corridor. A female Antisian, a race of beings that split the difference between Lizard and Human, walked out into the pit clad in battle armor. As she held her one-handed sword high in the air, the crowd reciprocated by way of cheers. As the guards removed the Second Plutonian from his shackles, he became unnerved, panicking as the reality of his situation set in. "You can't do this to me!" shouted the meek and frightened Second Plutonian as he was handed his broadsword and pushed out into the battlefield, where the Antisian was waiting with an unmistakable grin. The Second Plutonian attempted to hold his sword out in front of him, but the weight of the weapon caused him to fall forward in his attempts, much to the amusement of the audience, and the Antisian as well. Skeeter, having seen this dance plenty of times before, grabbed the chains of the slaves with a look of exasperation and defeat, and continued with the group of Recruits back towards their respective corridor. There was more laughter outside as Skeeter and the Recruits marched back into the corridor, where he opened the gate, once again corralling the creatures into their holding pen, but this time entering with them.

Outside, the crowd continued to get an enjoyable kick out of the sight of a Second Plutonian running around the pit in fear for his life, having abandoned his weapon long ago. The impact of the sobs of a Second Plutonian – a torturous wail if ever there was one – seemed lost on the spectators.

Back in the left corridor, Skeeter stood in front of the Human woman, addressing her directly for the first time since she entered the pen.

"Who are you?" he asked her.

"I can't tell you that," the woman replied.

"Why not?" Skeeter demanded.

"It is not how the prophecy unfolds," she explained matter-of-factly.

"The prophecy? What prophecy?" he asked.

"The one that foretells the fate of my people; the inhabitants of Temeculon," the woman responded.

"The fate of your people?" responded Skeeter incredulously. "Listen lady, I don't know who you think I am, but I'm telling you, you've hitched your wagon to the wrong ox here."

"No," she declared flatly. "I haven't."

Skeeter looked into her eyes intensely, searching for some hint of insanity or psychological trauma. On the contrary, he found only steely determination and considerable intellect.

After several moments spent searching his memory banks to no avail, Skeeter gave up and retreated back towards the outside of the pen.

"Please, you must remember," she called to him as he walked away.

Outside, the Second Plutonian was cornered and the Antisian was advancing on him, her sword held high in the air. As she approached the cowering being, she drove her sword directly through his chest, causing a blue vapor to emanate from the open wound. As the colored vapor rushed out of the Second Plutonian's body, the being deflated into nothingness, and the crowd cheered in approval. As the Antisian played to the crowd with her sword held high, welcoming more and more applause, a single guard rushed out and retrieved the body of the dead Second Plutonian, which was no larger in mass than a shriveled balloon.

Standing from her chair positioned among the more powerful of those in attendance, Ambassador Elocusia walked back into the center of the pit, addressing the crowd.

"We have just witnessed the staggering brilliance of the Antisian form in full effect, a testament to the living miracle of Creation. Additionally, we honor the sacrifice of the Second Plutonian in the name of the Glory of Life and Being."

"All hail the Second Plutonian!" the crowd responded in unison.

Ambassador Elocusia nodded once again to the guards on her left, who commenced with the custom of banging their weapons against each other three times, signaling the next battle was ready to take place.

With another heavy sigh, Skeeter picked up the chains.

"Here we go again, guys," he remarked.

Even the Arachneophyte looked depressed and defeated as he began to realize there was a legitimate chance of his demise. Only Skeeter knew that the creature would be the one with the best odds of survival. As the man led the Recruits out once again through the corridor and past the guards onto the battlefield, the crowd again took advantage of the opportunity to show their enthusiasm for the proceedings thus far.

"These beings love themselves some death, don't they?" Skeeter thought to himself.

It was not the first time such a notion had crossed his mind.

With the Recruits having returned to their rightful place in the middle of the battlefield, the next Esteemed Representative was called out to the pit by the Ambassador.

"Please join me in welcoming our next Esteemed Representative, Novak Greshultimanth, Prince of Quentrasion, and son to Morescenallio." The Ambassador bowed gracefully as the Prince strode out to meet her, offering her a kiss on the cheek which she returned with a sly smile. She returned to her chair, and continued to look upon the Prince as he strolled up and down the line of Recruits, peering into the eyes of each and every possible participant in the next battle. As he reached the end of the row and stared into the eyes of the Arachneophyte, the creature became aggressive, hissing and scratching its many legs against the ground. The Prince smiled, amused by the creature's reaction, and took a deliberate step back before raising his hand slowly towards the Arachneophyte. The crowd gasped and spoke to one another in hushed murmurs.

"The Arachneophyte. Didn't see that coming," Skeeter thought to himself. *"Even after all these years, the Olympiad can still shock, it seems."*

Even The Overseer, in his silent but ever-present watch, stirred and let out a slow groan that coursed throughout the walls of the stadium. The guards looked at each other in hesitation, each waiting for the other to take the lead in unshackling the Arachneophyte. As one of the guards gathered up the courage and began to approach, the creature became hostile, swiping at the guards and resisting their advances. Once again, the Arachneophyte caught the attention of The Overseer, who, growing weary of the creature's act, raised a gargantuan foot mere feet off of the ground and slowly smashed it down, causing an impact near that of a seismic tremor that reverberated throughout the structure of the arena, and shook the grounds of the pit. The Overseer huffed through his nose, sending a dry wind across the battlefield that kicked up dust and debris. The Arachneophyte turned upwards at The Overseer with an expression of resigned submission that indicated he understood his fate. It was the same expression held by the creature's indentured compatriots. Without resistance, the guards unshackled the multi-legged creature, who when presented with the available weaponry, angrily knocked the rack down, taking insult to the idea that he should need a weapon to stand a chance in battle.

As Skeeter walked over and took hold of the chains, he found himself near to the Human woman, who wore an expression of impatience.

"We haven't much time," she said under her breath.

"I told you, I don't know what you're talking about," Skeeter said in an exasperated half-whisper that caused several of the guards to look at him with a curious eye. He proceeded to pull ahead of the group of intergalactic refugees, leading them back into the left corridor, and into the holding pen. As he led them in and began to close the gate, she pleaded with him aloud.

"Please, you mustn't resist," she exclaimed. "The prophecy foretells of my people's destiny, and you are the key. You."

"If it's so damned important, just tell me who I am!" yelled Skeeter, finally having lost his patience in the matter. "You sit here and cry to me about the fate of your people and blah, blah, blah, and you clearly know who I am, and what my role in this whole supposed prophecy is, and yet you won't just tell me so we can put this whole damn thing to rest!"

"The prophecy…" she said in defeat.

"You and your damned prophecy!" Skeeter angrily replied. "I'm sorry to tell you this, sweetie, but I think you may have lost your mind."

"The prophecy…" was all the woman could meekly muster up in response as she stared off into the distance at nothing in particular.

Outside, the Arachneophyte was currently doing battle with an Ogrishian, a race of wolf-like creatures revered for their vigilance in battle, and celebrated for their ability to do battle on both two and four legs, providing a distinct strategic advantage in the form of positional flexibility. For some moments, it looked as though the Arachneophyte had the upper hand, and would be able to do the Ogrishian in. However, one slight miscalculation resulted in three of the eight available appendages writhing on the ground, separated from the rest of the creature's body. The Ogrishian, having been on the wrong side of this match several times, wasted no time with outward displays of panache, and quickly drove his sword through the brain of the creature as soon as the appropriate moment presented itself. The crowd, as it had done so many times before, thundered with rapturous applause, giving a standing ovation to the Ogrishian for such an entertaining display as no less than four guards rushed out to the battlefield to carry the body of the Arachneophyte away.

Ambassador Elocusia finished her small talk with the Prince of Quentrasion, who had recently been moved at the Ambassador's request and was now seated next to her, then rose from her chair, and returned to the center of the battle pit to introduce the next Esteemed Representative.

"As we stand here in awe of the might and grace displayed by the Ogrishian, we once again honor the fallen by showing our respects to the Arachneophyte for allowing us to bask in the brilliance of the Glory of Life and Being."

"All hail the Arachneophyte!" the crowd announced.

One glance from the Ambassador and three clangs of the axe later, Skeeter again resumed his position from within the corridor, grabbing hold of the chains, and leading the five remaining Recruits out into the middle of the arena. The Human woman was now reduced to a shell of the person who had stood proud and defiant at the beginning of the games.

"Sooner or later, everyone breaks. They all do. Don't be too hard on yourself, sweetie," he thought to himself as he looked back to see the woman trudging through the dirt with calloused feet and broken will. For several moments throughout the day, Skeeter had wished that her words were true; that he was some intergalactic hero destined to break the shackles of an oppressed group of beings. Or whatever

the hell this prophecy of hers foretold. Anything would be better than the current life that he had been forced into.

"Our next Esteemed Representative is Lady Contrascoria," continued Ambassador Elocusia, "Queen of the Fragellan Nebula, and daughter to the late Lord Duracosis. Please welcome her with the same sense of civility and grace you have shone upon our previous Representatives." The ambassador returned to her chair as the Fragellan Queen took center stage in the pit. She disdainfully looked over the ragged and worn group of Recruits, now reduced to two humans, one Second Plutonian, one Acriot, and one Cartrellion. None of them looked as though they would put up much of a fight in battle at this point.

The Queen paid little regard to the choices in front of her, and wore an unimpressed expression across her face as she strode in front of the Recruits, looking them up and down and finding herself with the same recurring sense of pity; regardless of whom she chose to do battle with her warrior, it was certain to be a tepid and uninspiring affair. More casually than the previous Representatives, she took the customary step backward, and with a certain lack of drama and flare, pointed at the Human woman, whom the Esteemed Representative could see repeatedly mouthing a silent word she could not identify.

The woman seemed unaware at first, but as the guards approached her, she snapped out her self-induced hypnosis to see Lady Contrascoria pointing at her, and the crowd that seemed to slip into oblivion just moments ago, could now be heard filling the stadium with the excited cheers of those about to witness a bloodbath. As the immediacy of the situation hit the woman's consciousness, she began to panic. The guards attempted to take off her chains and she resisted. Guards came on either side and restrained her arms as she thrashed about, kicking and wailing, as another guard went to unshackle the chain around her neck. It was this moment that triggered a response in Skeeter; a recollection of past events. Suddenly everything made sense, and Skeeter remembered who this woman was to have put so much faith in him. He had seen this image before. Sure, the settings and certain characters were different, but he had seen this exact image play out before him, albeit in the chambers of the King of Temeculon, and while the woman before him was the same one he had seen decades ago, the physical perfections of youth and privilege had since made way for the weathered ravages of time and hardship.

As a young man, Skeeter had developed a reputation as a talented and promising individual, tough in negotiations, and technically skilled in both surveillance and the art of Extraction; sneaking in and rescuing prisoners who had been kidnapped, typically for money or some measure of political influence. After successfully completing several missions-for-hire for Atwood Marghatran, he had developed a strong bond with the King of Temeculon, as well as his two daughters, Sheera and Madrissa, and his wife, Queen Esracoscia. When not under any particular contract or mission, it was not uncommon for Skeeter to join the family for meals and extended stays. The Marghatran family was always more than happy to accommodate, and although Skeeter never expressed any romantic interest in the king's daughters, Atwood Marghatran always secretly hoped that the young man would marry into the family. Any father wants a good man for his daughter when she is of age, and Skeeter had proven time and again to be a good man, which seemed in short supply anymore to Atwood.

One day, Skeeter and several other contractors hired for a surveillance mission were congregating in the King's chambers, who insisted that his family be present during all such discussions. Atwood may have been surrounded by three woman on a constant basis, and it occurred to him on more than one occasion that this may account for his feeling of admiration towards Skeeter, but at no point did he ever put his daughters or his wife below himself, and he always became agitated when people insinuated that his daughters may not be fit for the eventual throne. After several such exchanges early in his career, it became common knowledge that to question the abilities or potential of Atwood's daughters to effectively rule the nation was a quick and effective way to lose favor with the King of Temeculon.

As Skeeter was disseminating information to the King and his family, there was a swift and sudden coup that took place, staged by one of King Atwood's most trusted advisors, known simply as Artimus. After falling into discussions with the wrong people, Artimus was given an incredible fortune to dethrone Atwood Marghatran. Artimus continued to serve as trusted advisor to the man that paid him, Lechreon Vildegraaten, who immediately took over the throne and began a decades-long rule that would be recorded in history as one of the most brutal since King Nero of Earth so many years ago. Although the King, his daughters, and his wife were sentenced to lifelong imprisonment, Artimus and Vildegraaten had other plans for Skeeter, recognizing him as the young man celebrated for his Extraction skills. They gave Skeeter a choice between death and a life spent serving as Artimus' hand, watching over the advisors' slaves and conducting his business transactions for him. Really, it was no choice at all.

Shame. Shame was the emotion Skeeter could most remember in that moment. Shame that he had been so foolish; so lacking in the perception that he was appropriately celebrated for. Like so many men before him, and many that would come after, Skeeter had let his guard down because of the comfort he felt around this family. He would go on to wrestle with this for many years, not just for having let down the closest thing to family he had ever known, but also failing to resolve the merit of being surrounded by family if you cannot truly enjoy their company. And now, as the guards grabbed hold of the woman, wrestling her out of the chains, he could see her as a young teenager, resisting the hired guards of the once trusted advisor, kicking at their bodies and spitting at their faces in youthful rebellion. Skeeter could only wonder about the path that eventually led her to the battleground upon which they currently stood. Suddenly, his entire history with the family flashed before him in the smallest of moments, and he knew what he had to do.

"Halt!" Skeeter announced at the top of his lungs. It was enough to startle the guards, who held off on wrestling with the woman for at least a few moments to look up at him.

"What is the meaning of this interruption?" demanded Lady Contrascoria.

"I, John "Skeeter" Perrison, invoke Article 29 as outlined in the Sacred Parchment of the Olympiad," Skeeter declared.

The crowd loudly murmured among one another, no one seemingly familiar with the language of Article 29. Ambassador Elocusia stood and impatiently addressed the man responsible for managing the Recruits.

"Article 29? What is the meaning of this?!" the Ambassador demanded.

"Article 29 dictates no reasoning be necessitated or even considered; merely volunteering is proof enough of one's vigilance in their beliefs," Skeeter explained.

"Article 29 is outdated; written during a time when the Olympiad was a much different tournament, with much different rules," the Ambassador curtly responded.

"It is my understanding that no Amendment has ever been written into law regarding Article 29, is that not correct?" inquired Skeeter.

The silent response from the Ambassador was as much a confirmation as any words she could have invoked.

"Very well," the Ambassador responded, before turning around to address the crowd. "It is under the ever-watchful eye of the Universe that I, Ambassador Elocusia of the Acriotic nation, do announce that the Human woman is pardoned and hereby barred from participating in this years' tournament, as is decreed within the Sacred Parchment of the Olympiad. John Perrison of Earth will take her place on the battlefield."

The crowd was stunned. Audible gasps were heard, with many spectators in shock. Even The Overseer rustled from his position outside of the arena, if only a bit. Never before had such precedence been set at the Olympiad, and the audience could only wonder why John Perrison had made such a sacrifice on the woman's behalf. Some speculated that Skeeter had grown romantically involved with the woman during their brief time alone in the corridor. Others merely resolved that the man had a death wish, and could carry on with his existence no longer. Whatever the reason, the crowd agreed that the last minute replacement would make for a much more entertaining battle.

Despite the obvious annoyance implied by her body language, Lady Contrascoria made the customary glance to the right corridor as the guards clanged their weapons against each other to signal the warrior to enter the battlefield. Guards rushed out to the pit carrying the rack of available weaponry for Skeeter to choose from.

"What have I just done?" thought Skeeter.

As he looked over his choices, he remembered his time with the Marghatran family, and as he thought about King Atwood, a warmth came over him, and he knew that somewhere, somehow, the King shone his approval down upon him.

As Skeeter considered his options, Lady Contrascoria's warrior marched out of the right corridor, an immense cyclops wielding a giant spiked club.

"Well," Skeeter thought to himself, *"at least they'll be able to say you were an honorable man as they stand over your corpse."*

The Cyclops stood tall and strong, the ground quivering ever so slightly with each step as the mountainous creature progressed towards center stage. As the Cyclops reached its place in the pit, Skeeter took one look into the creature's enormous eye. It possessed a sense of duty; one that said he would not fail in his objective to destroy anyone standing in front of him.

"And that person will be me," Skeeter told himself matter-of-factly.

Skeeter turned away from the being and considered his weaponry options. A sword would do no good, as this was not a battle that would be won at close range. Not by him, anyways. The long-range battle-axe was a more appropriate piece of equipment given Skeeter's approach, but such a hefty and unwieldy weapon would slow him down. Skeeter was of the opinion that the best way to counter strength was with intellect and speed. After dismissing several other options, Skeeter settled on a traditional bow and arrow.

The crowd was amused by Skeeter's choice of weaponry. The bow and arrow was seen mostly as a nod to history; no legitimate contender had even so much as fought with a bow and arrow, let alone rose victorious in battle. Still,

Skeeter knew that if he was to win this fight, he would have to use a long-range approach, regardless of how much the crowd may or may not approve. As he grabbed for the bow and a satchel of arrows, the Cyclops emitted a mocking chuckle.

The guards all scattered back to their respective corridors as the Ambassador and Esteemed Representative took their seats, leaving Skeeter and the Cyclops alone in the middle of the battlefield. Skeeter stared at the Cyclops deep into his lone eye. If he was to stand any chance, he knew he could not allow the enormous creature to perceive his fear.

After several moments locked in a stare-down, the Cyclops twitched ever so slightly as he put his initial attack into motion, swinging his club high overhead with the intent of bringing it straight down on Skeeter. As the club arched through the air, Skeeter rolled to his right, displaying a swift grace to his movements. The spikes of the club clanged against the packed dirt as they collided, and a tuft of dust kicked into the air.

Skeeter, pointed squarely at the creature, walked backwards as he fired off three arrows into the primary arm of the Cyclops. The Cyclops let out a small wince, but quickly broke the arrows off of his arm and cast them aside. As the creature turned to look at Skeeter, he paused and smiled, letting the man know that his arrows caused little harm or pain to his enormous size. Skeeter, never one for showboating during a match, quickly fired off an arrow that landed straight in the Cyclops' bottom lip, causing the creature to emit a deep groan that surprised the audience. The sensitive tissue of the lips whereupon the arrow had lodged itself seemed to get more of the response Skeeter was looking for.

The Cyclops, unaccustomed to such pain, took offense to to act, and quickly yanked the arrow from his lip, casting it aside in anger. The creature's breathing had increased dramatically, and Skeeter knew it was time to take up the defensive. The Cyclops panted heavily, allowing his anger to take over. With a large battle cry that echoed throughout the arena, even stirring The Overseer a touch, the Cyclops charged full-speed ahead towards Skeeter. As he was within a dozen feet of the man, the Cyclops reached his right arm as far back as it would go and swung his club, hoping the parallel arc would smash the small human to pieces upon impact. Skeeter, holding his position, quickly fired off another two arrows directly into the giants elbow and rolled forward through the giant creature's legs. The cyclops whiffed his club and stumbled forward, much to the amusement of the audience. Hunched over the ground, the Cyclops looked back between his legs to see Skeeter standing confidently behind him, awaiting his next move. The Cyclops, realizing he would have to be more cunning with this combatant, swiftly kicked his right leg backwards, making direct contact with Skeeter's chest and sending him

Skeeter knew that if he was to win this fight, he would have to use a long-range approach, regardless of how much the crowd may or may not approve. As he grabbed for the bow and a satchel of arrows, the Cyclops emitted a mocking chuckle.

The guards all scattered back to their respective corridors as the Ambassador and Esteemed Representative took their seats, leaving Skeeter and the Cyclops alone in the middle of the battlefield. Skeeter stared at the Cyclops deep into his lone eye. If he was to stand any chance, he knew he could not allow the enormous creature to perceive his fear.

After several moments locked in a stare-down, the Cyclops twitched ever so slightly as he put his initial attack into motion, swinging his club high overhead with the intent of bringing it straight down on Skeeter. As the club arched through the air, Skeeter rolled to his right, displaying a swift grace to his movements. The spikes of the club clanged against the packed dirt as they collided, and a tuft of dust kicked into the air.

Skeeter, pointed squarely at the creature, walked backwards as he fired off three arrows into the primary arm of the Cyclops. The Cyclops let out a small wince, but quickly broke the arrows off of his arm and cast them aside. As the creature turned to look at Skeeter, he paused and smiled, letting the man know that his arrows caused little harm or pain to his enormous size. Skeeter, never one for showboating during a match, quickly fired off an arrow that landed straight in the Cyclops' bottom lip, causing the creature to emit a deep groan that surprised the audience. The sensitive tissue of the lips whereupon the arrow had lodged itself seemed to get more of the response Skeeter was looking for.

The Cyclops, unaccustomed to such pain, took offense to to act, and quickly yanked the arrow from his lip, casting it aside in anger. The creature's breathing had increased dramatically, and Skeeter knew it was time to take up the defensive. The Cyclops panted heavily, allowing his anger to take over. With a large battle cry that echoed throughout the arena, even stirring The Overseer a touch, the Cyclops charged full-speed ahead towards Skeeter. As he was within a dozen feet of the man, the Cyclops reached his right arm as far back as it would go and swung his club, hoping the parallel arc would smash the small human to pieces upon impact. Skeeter, holding his position, quickly fired off another two arrows directly into the giants elbow and rolled forward through the giant creature's legs. The cyclops whiffed his club and stumbled forward, much to the amusement of the audience. Hunched over the ground, the Cyclops looked back between his legs to see Skeeter standing confidently behind him, awaiting his next move. The Cyclops, realizing he would have to be more cunning with this combatant, swiftly kicked his right leg backwards, making direct contact with Skeeter's chest and sending him flying backwards several dozen feet. The crowd, again, found this sight amusing.

As Skeeter sat on the ground, clutching his chest and gasping for air, the Cyclops slowly picked his large body off of the ground. He turned and stared directly at Skeeter, knowing the time to strike was upon him. The Cyclops positioned himself in a two-point stance, harnessing all of his body's potential energy that would in a brief moment turn kinetic. His vision blurry, Skeeter drew in breath as best he could, and as the image in front of him came into focus, he could immediately see that a life-or-death moment had presented itself. He tried to pick his body up, but it would not allow him to. The Cyclops charged forth, again wailing its huge battle cry as the creature charged directly at Skeeter. Skeeter looked to his left and saw nothing. Quickly, he turned right and saw the bow just out of arms reach. As the Cyclops continued its aggressive charge, Skeeter reached his right hand as far as it would allow; he was mere fingertips away from grabbing hold of the bow.

The Cyclops was advancing rapidly, his spiked club held high in the air. Spectators gasped and stood, pointing at the Human man who was moments away from death. With his last ounce of effort, will, and strength, Skeeter stretched his fingers out the additional half-inch necessary to feel the smooth wooden texture of the bow. Sliding the weapon towards him with his middle finger, he outstretched his hand and could now grasp the weapon in its totality. As the Cyclops began to bring the club down towards Skeeter, the man swiftly grabbed hold of the bow, and fired three arrows straight into the eye of the Cyclops. The Cyclops was stopped dead in its tracks. It hesitated, the creature's biology catching up to what had just taken place. After the initial moment of shock, the creature allowed the club to fall from his hands and reached up, covering its face with its hands. It grabbed haphazardly at the air, trying to remove the arrows from its eye, though it now completely lacked for vision. The creature drunkenly stumbled across the battlefield, swinging its large arms to and fro in a vain attempt to regain its sight. Finally, after one last failed attempt, the creature lost consciousness and fell to the ground with a large thud, kicking up dirt and rocks around its fallen body. After a long, silent moment of shock, the crowd erupted in applause as Skeeter looked around, confused and not exactly processing the moment in its entirety.

From the outside of the pit, the Human woman smiled an effervescent smile. She closed her eyes, relishing the moment that her prophecy came true, and held her head to the sky before beginning to hum a melody from her childhood; a melody that had been all but forgotten, buried beneath the sands of time.

There was a crack of thunder in the day sky that captured the attention of all in attendance, Skeeter and The Overseer included. As the crowd looked up, the sky began to change from the bright baby blue that had canvassed the sky, to a darker shade of grey. Commotion began among the spectators, and clouds rolled in from either side of the sky, flanking the blue and swallowing it whole. Lightning seemed to crash from within the ever-present grey clouds, themselves turning the sky darker and darker, blue giving way to grey giving way to black. Within several moments, what was recently a pitch-perfect day had turned into ominous night. As Skeeter looked around at the darkened sky, the spectators afraid and uncertain, he glanced towards the woman, standing among the other slaves, smiling wide, with her eyes closed and head to the sky. It occurred to him that perhaps the woman had indeed lost her sanity. Skeeter then turned his attention to The Overseer, who himself had his large boulder of a head turned upwards towards the darkened sky.

Before long, there was an audible rumbling coming from above, low at first, but distinctly noticeable. It continued to grow louder and more severe with each passing moment, the thunder and lightning ever-increasing. The rumbling had now gotten to be so intense that the vibrations were causing the structure of the arena to shake, causing several spectators to shout in surprise and fear. The stadium was vibrating as though there were a long, sustained earthquake in progress. Pieces of the stadium began to collapse and fall to the ground. The Overseer himself seemed to be losing pieces of his own mass as he began to slowly rise to his feet.

As Skeeter stood, his legs braced as tightly to the ground as physics would allow, he looked upwards as the clouds above them parted and an enormous metallic silver structure broke through the sky and into his vision.

As the structure continued its descent to the ground, a large white-yellow light was cast upon the people in the stadium, and the blue of the day's sky peaked through the curtains of the grey storm clouds behind the giant silver spacecraft that had revealed itself.

The massive structure hung overhead, hovering in place only several stories above the highest point of the stadium, and above The Overseer as well, who had finished his ascent and was standing upright. The Overseer slowly turned his head from the sky and downward until he was staring directly at Skeeter, who was standing alone in the center of the pit, staring back at him. The Overseer laboriously extended his arm down into the middle of the pit, his palm lying upward in the battlefield. The Overseer was silent as he stared at Skeeter.

As Skeeter stood there, uncertain as of what to do next, he was joined by the Human woman, Madrissa.

"I knew you would come through for me and my people," explained Madrissa Marghatran, "I knew the prophecy would be as foretold."

"What is this?" asked Skeeter. "What's going on?"

"This is you showing your true character, the strength of character that my family and I were privileged enough to be exposed to. This is you reclaiming your life."

"I don't understand," Skeeter replied.

"Several years after my family and I were imprisoned by Artimus and Vildegraaten, I managed to escape. I went into hiding for several years, carefully plotting the moves and forming the allegiances that would enable me after many years to overthrow the corrupt regime of Artimus and Vildegraaten, and free my family.

"King Atwood...He's free?" asked Skeeter.

"Yes," affirmed Madrissa, "as are Sheera and Mother."

Skeeter felt a joy and relief deep within himself; a satisfaction of knowing that he had followed his true purpose, and that by the light and strength of his character, he had done his part to help a good man in his efforts to rule his kingdom with justice and a fair hand.

"So where do we go now?" Skeeter asked.

"Back home to Temeculon," confirmed Madrissa. "My father, King Atwood, is in need of a trustworthy individual to fill the recently vacated role of advisor to the throne. He can think of no better candidate than you. Come."

Madrissa grabbed Skeeter's hand and led him up into the hand of The Overseer. After safely making their way to the middle of The Overseer's palm, the mountainous boulder of a being raised his arm and lifted the two Humans to the sky until they were staring directly at the side of the immense spacecraft. An open hatch revealed King Atwood, standing with his wife and his daughter by his side.

"King Atwood," Skeeter continued, "I truly never imagined this day would come; the day when we would be reunited."

"Welcome home, my son," the King responded, "Welcome home."

Remote Viewer

by Rob Watson

"These fuckers mean business," Cole Morrison says to himself as he hovers above several scientists in the Nakatomi Research and Development main laboratory. His mental projection goes unnoticed by the workers below, a formless body of consciousness that is invisible to everyone, including himself. "This new chip will revolutionize the industry."

Cole's mental projection exits the lab. His speed steadily increases as he goes upward and out through the roof, piercing the pure blue sky and soaring through the clouds.

His speed slows as he reaches his destination, his physical body lying in a darkened lab inside Steele Technologies. "I can never get used to this shit", he thinks to himself as he nears his lifeless body, itself connected to a myriad of wires and electrodes. As Cole's mental projection enters his body, his heart rate, pulse, and brain waves increase. Movement comes to his lifeless body. After gasping a big breath, Cole grabs hold of the ring on his right pinky, a white gold band with a two carat diamond in the center. He smiles as the technicians come forward and remove the electrodes.

Cole finishes dressing and heads up to the penthouse office suite. He brushes past the receptionist and enters the office of Sidney Steele, the CEO of Steele Industries.

"Is it as bad as we thought?" Sid asks.

"It's worse, Boss," Cole replies as he approaches the front of the CEO's desk. "You're holding a big shit sandwich and there's no one else that'll take a bite."

Sid picks up the phone and buzzes his secretary. "Linda, the emergency board meeting is confirmed! Ten o'clock sharp!" Sid slams the phone down, stands up, and walks over to the window.

Cole joins Sid who is staring at the waves caressing the beach below.

"That look on your face makes me long for the old days when I was fly spying for CIA," says Cole. "Back then I was just peeping on sweaty Soviets buried in silos with their fingers next to launch buttons. But then again that new Japanese chip is kinda like an ICBM with its sights set on Steele Technologies."

"Thanks for that insightful metaphor."

"That was a simile, Sydney."

"Well, whatever the fuck it was, it was pretty damn accurate," replies Sid as he walks back over to his desk.

"And your accuracy rating was what, ninety-two, ninety-three percent?"

"Ninety-seven point one. No other fly-spy got past eighty-five, ever! I was their golden boy, the best of the best. That's why they gave me this ring," says Cole as he grabs his pinky finger.

"Yeah you're good, I'll admit that, but. . ."

"But what," asks Cole.

Sid clears his throat. "Well, as a 'non-viewer' I've always wondered if you ever been afraid you wouldn't find your way back to your body after one of your little jaunts across the stratosphere someday?"

"No way. I'm part homing pigeon, and this ring is my beacon," Cole says, playing with his ring. "It can get weird sometimes, though."

"Yeah, how much weirder can it get?" Sid asks facetiously.

Cole snickers. "I'm starting to take journeys in my sleep," he answers. "And once on the ceiling of the Nakatomi board room, I could swear I was making the chandelier move."

"Look Cole, if you want some time off. . ."

"I'm not shitting you, Sid. A couple of missions ago, I was hovering close to the board-room ceiling, and I drifted towards this big-ass chandelier in the middle of the room. It reminded me of the one hanging in the ballroom of the Hotel Bristol, where my Junior year homecoming dance was held. Have I ever told you this story?"

"Nope," Sid answers as sits down at his desk and packs tobacco into his pipe.

"Figures. It's a part of my life I'd rather forget." Cole goes to the bar and takes a cube out of the ice bucket. "Let's just say that I don't look back at my high school years as being the best time of my life." Cole tosses up the ice cube and grabs it mid-air. "I was a misfit, the class weirdo that even the fat and ugly girls wouldn't be caught dating."

Sid lights his pipe. "Hey, so was I, and look how I turned out."

Cole hesitates for a moment, then continues, "So it's my Junior year, and after two and a half dateless years, my family are starting to wonder about my sexual orientation. I knew I wouldn't get a date for prom, so I decided to go stag to the homecoming dance and tell my parents that I was taking Kimberly Turner, this gorgeous red head I had a hard-on for since the third grade. So there I am in my dad's shoes and the corduroy suit my mom bought me for our family portraits the year before, when up comes Kimberly Turner. She asked me if I wanted to dance. My mouth was so dry that I couldn't answer, so I nodded. She led me to the middle of the dance floor. The lights were low, and a slow song was playing. She pulled me close and pressed her body against mine. I remember thinking how glad I was that I was wearing those tight corduroy slacks so that Kimberly wouldn't be jabbed by the huge boner building inside my boxers. I could hardly believe it when her hands slowly reached down, unfastened my belt, unbuttoned my button, and unzipped my fly. Then, just as I was pledging to sacrifice my first-born son to God for this impromptu hand-job from the girl of my dreams, the music stops and the lights turn up as three Neanderthals from the wrestling team, one of them being Kimberly's boyfriend, grab me from behind and pull down my pants."

"Fuck me..." Sid says as he shakes his head in disbelief.

"No, fuck me, as I'm standing there with a major erection peeking out of my boxers towards the student body and alumni of my alma mater."

Sid turns his head to conceal the grin struggling to burst through onto his face.

"And as if that wasn't humiliating enough, as I bend down to pull up my pants, I lose balance and fall down on my back, with my dick acting as a tent pole for my white boxers. As I lay there amidst the of laughter and crude remarks, I all could do was focus on the crystal chandelier hanging on the ceiling above me." Cole tosses up the ice cube and catches it in his cupped hand. "I couldn't transfer to another school, not unless my parents moved. So I had to endure a year and a half of daily ridicule for what happened that night.

Sid squirms in his chair as an uneasy silence fills the room. After a few moments, he clears his throat and sits up. "I'm sorry, all this has to do with what?"

"Nakatomi, the chandelier. . .

"Oh yes, the chandelier," Sid says as he re-lights his pipe. "Go ahead," says Sid as he watches Cole squeeze the ice cube between his palms. "Tell me about the Nakatomi chandelier."

"First, I have to brief you on the basics of mental projection. This might be hard for you to understand since you're not a viewer, so I'll try to put it in layman's terms. When I project, I'm disengaged; separated from my body."

"No shit?" says Sid sarcastically as he takes a long draw from his pipe.

"Don't be stupid, Sid. What I mean is that it's not like the movies where a spirit has form and can see themselves and their hands and their feet and whatever. It's not even like the way we see; it's hard to describe. It's just like you're there. You know how insects have multiple eyes and can see at a wide angle? Well, this is more than that. It's like I can see everything in the room all at once." Cole raises his voice as he notices Sid's attention waning. "So as I hovered in the Nakatomi boardroom, seething as the chandelier reminded me of the homecoming dance, I focused my attention on one single crystal of the chandelier. As I focused all my energies on that one crystal, it's as if my perspective narrowed from my three hundred and sixty degree view down to that one crystal on the chandelier and nothing else. My vision narrowed even more, to the size of a pinpoint, and the crystal burst into hundreds of pieces, raining down on the boardroom table, scaring the shit out of everyone in the place." Cole throws the half melted ice cube back into the bucket.

"Wow, Cole, that's some kind of story."

"You ain't heard nothing yet. One night I dreamt I was looking through our photo albums. The next morning, when I awoke and went downstairs the photo albums were off of the shelves and strewn all over the floor. My wife swore she hadn't touched them."

Sid shakes his head. "That's something, Cole. Sounds like a Twilight Zone episode I once saw."

"Funny guy. So far this psychokinesis has only occurred when I'm viewing or dreaming. I don't have that ability when I'm conscious and in my body."

"Remind me to take you to Vegas sometime." Sid knocks the ashes out of his pipe and then looks at Cole. "Have time to come over to my house this afternoon?"

Cole looks over at Sid. "Your house?"

"So we can hide all my valuables in a warehouse somewhere before my creditors put liens on them when Nakatomi starts screwing me."

"I don't think Katie will approve. You know how much she loves to show off your art collection."

"Katie can take a flying fuck. Then again, she probably already has."

Cole picks up Katie's pictures off of Sid's desk. "I thought you had the perfect marriage."

"I did," answers Sid.

Cole winces. "So what happened?"

Sid takes the picture from Cole, then walks over to the bar and pours himself a neat scotch. "People change. At first we were so into each other, practically inseparable. Then I started to spend more and more time at the office, and she spent more and more time eyeing the pool man." Sid downs the rest of his drink, and then throws the empty glass against the wall. "Now it's five years later and my blushing bride has become a shameless whore that'll screw anyone who knocks on the door." Sid slams his wife's picture face down on top of the bar.

"Why don't you divorce the cheating bitch?" Cole asks.

"I would, but the trouble is I can't prove anything. So if I divorce her, she'll take half of everything. Man, I wish I had your sight, then I could nail her tits to the wall. You must be a smug bastard being able to check on your wife and make sure she's not screwing you over. Not that she would."

"Yeah, not that she would." Cole reaches with his right hand and takes his wedding band between his middle finger and his thumb and rubs it. "I have a real winner."

"Well I'm glad one of us has it good." Sid walks over and puts his hand on Cole's shoulder. "I guess you can take the rest of the week off. How long has it been since you've seen your wife, or had a good night's sleep?"

Cole ponders Sid's question for a moment. "Two and a half weeks."

Sid's eyes widen. "Shit! How much are you going to bill me?"

"Enough to pay for my second honeymoon," Cole says with a smile.

"Well enjoy it, buddy, you've more than earned it." Sid puts his pipe down in the ashtray.
"See you later. I have to go home and think of a way to save my corporate ass." Sid picks up the
attaché from his desk. "Lock the door on your way out."

"Good luck", says Cole as he salutes Sid.

"Thanks, I need it," answers Sid. He returns Cole's salute and exits his office.

Cole walks over to the window and stares out toward the ocean with Sid's words still lingering on his mind. He started thinking about all the time he spends away from home, about all the broken promises; all the missed rendezvous'. Cole looks over at Sid's chair, a high-backed, leather-clad executive chair with padded armrests. He reaches into his pocket and takes out his billfold. Cole flips to the picture of his wife and stares longingly at it. He takes it out of the plastic holder and looks at the back.

"To Cole, from Faith. Always."

Cole doesn't have to read the inscription to know what it says, for these words are engraved in his heart. They are the words from his college sweetheart, his one and only love. Cole re-inserts the picture, puts the billfold back into his pocket and starts toward the door.

Suddenly, Sid's words flash into Cole's head, "How long has it been since you've seen your wife…People change…I wish I had your sight. . ." Cole looks over at Sid's chair, looks back at the office door, then walks around the desk and plops into the chair. "This is crazy. I have nothing to worry about. Still, better safe than sorry."

Cole reclines back and stretches out his feet, folding his hands over his chest. Within seconds his body is completely relaxed. Cole exits his body, goes up through the roof and heads home. He enters through the front door and goes up the stairs to the second floor. Suddenly the glint from polished bronze letters catch his gaze -- letters that form the words FOREVER, MY LOVE fastened above his and his wife's wedding portrait hanging beside their bedroom door.

"This is stupid!" Cole turns around and heads back out the front door.

As he makes his way to the front lawn, Cole notices his wife's car parked in the garage, next to a Harley Davidson motorcycle. "What the fuck?" Like a bullet, Cole transports his mind into his bedroom. The vision of his darling wife straddling atop a greasy tattooed biker hits him like a ton of bricks.

Cole screams; screams which go unheard by his wife and her lover. A feeling of betrayal engulfs him, a betrayal which he has not suffered since that dreaded homecoming dance. Then his suffering transforms into rage, a rage which narrows his perspective down to only his wife and her lover. To Cole, only his wife and this man exist in this universe. His rage enables him to physically feel their bodies, as if he was physically in bed with them, disgusting Cole beyond measure. He rapidly changes his point of view to his wedding picture. His perspective narrows to a pinpoint. At that instant, the picture explodes, only to fall upon the deaf ears of the two engrossed lovers. "God damn you both! You may not hear me now, but you will! You both will!"

Cole returns to Steele Technologies and re-enters his body. He jumps to his feet, screaming maniacally, and proceeds to trash half of Sid's office. Afterwards, Cole sits amidst the mess he created. He checks his watch, then stands up and heads for the door. "No Sid, I won't fucking forget to lock the door." Cole exits, locks the door, and heads for home.

As Cole makes his way home, he has flashbacks of his wife and her lover in bed. He speeds dangerously along the dark winding road, narrowly avoiding several on-coming cars.

Cole screeches to a stop next to Faith's car. The motorcycle is nowhere to be seen. Cole enters the house. He makes his way upstairs to the master bedroom. He reaches the bedroom door, grabs the handle, and then pauses. "Wait a minute, if I kill the bitch now, it's capital murder. Let's just wait. Besides it won't be a party without Mr. Biker, so let us wait until tonight." Cole releases the door handle and goes downstairs.

Cole enters the den, turns on the fireplace and pours himself a cognac. He puts his drink upon a folded piece a paper on the cocktail table and sits down on the couch. Cole sits there, staring into nothingness while twisting round the ring on his little finger.

Early the next morning, Faith, Cole's buxom thirty-seven year-old wife, enters the den. The flames from the fireplace reflect off of her light green eyes as her wet brunette hair cascades over the bathrobe they stole from Club Med. Upon seeing Faith, Cole's emotions collide; love with hate, lust with revulsion.

"You didn't come to me last night," Faith says with a seductive voice. "I was waiting for you. Didn't you get my note?"

"No, I didn't," answers Cole angrily.

Faith walks over and puts her arms around him. "That's okay, it'll keep till tonight." Cole
pulls away as Faith tries to kiss him. "Now don't be grumpy. I'm sorry that I fell asleep, but you
didn't have to stay down here all night."

"No big deal," Cole says with a cold tone.

"Oh, before I forget, your sister-in-law wants to take us out to dinner tonight. You see, I have a little secret I've been keeping from you and she wants to be there to see the look on your face when I tell you."

"Yeah, knowing your sister I bet she does. Well, got to get dressed. Have to be in early today." Cole starts to get up.

"Come on lover, just a quick one. You know I get excited when you're away." Faith rubs Cole's chest.

"Yeah, but I didn't know how excited," Cole says to himself.

Faith continues to kiss and rub against Cole.

"What the hell, might as well do her before I 'do her'." Cole picks up his wife and carries her to the bedroom upstairs.

Cole enters the bedroom holding Faith in his arms. As she kisses his neck, Cole looks at
the messed up sheets on the bed. His ire flares as he has a flashback of the night before. Cole throws Faith onto the bed.

"Whoa cowboy, you got some fire in you this morning." Faith takes off her bathrobe, revealing her tanned naked body.

Cole stands next to the bed and undresses slowly, as several images of his wife and her lover flash before his eyes.

Faith squirms upon the sheets, becoming turned on more by the slow pace of Cole's disrobing. "If you're trying to drive me crazy, it's working."

Cole finishes undressing. He stands over his amorous wife, fingering his pinky ring in a Freudian fashion. He climbs unto the bed. He pulls Faith gently up to him, then throws her face down upon the bed and roughly mounts her, wrapping his hands firmly around her neck.

Faith's ecstatic moans and screams echo throughout the house. Cole pounds upon Faith with the fury of a man possessed. His anger magnifies with each flashback he has of Faith atop the biker. As the force of his pelvic thrusts increases, so heightens the level of Faith's gratification.

The ravishment continues until Faith crests her first wave of an ensuing orgasmic tsunami. She continues to squeal in sexual delight for some time after Cole has dismounted.

Cole lies down beside his wife. He stares at the ceiling wondering what the hell happened to his marriage. Exhausted from extreme mental anguish and lack of sleep, he closes his eyes.

Preparing for work, he hardly says a word to his wife. He is calm on the outside, but seething on the inside. As he leaves out the front door, Faith follows.

"Don't forget to come home early tonight, okay honey? I want some more of what I got this morning. . ."

"Don't worry, you'll get yours, you both will," Cole says under his breath as he drives away. Rage builds within Cole, which escalates all the way back to Steele Technologies. "Bitch, cunt, whore, bitch. . .I'll show them both."

Cole bursts through the lobby doors of Steele Technologies. The lobby guard starts to stand and offer a salutation, but after reading the expression on Cole's face, decides to sit back down and re-engage in his game of solitaire.

Cole approaches the elevator door, and presses the lobby button. He looks up to see that the elevator floor indicator reads eighteen. "Fuck it!" Cole heads toward the stairwell, bursting through the stairwell door and hurdling up the stairs.

He reaches the eighteenth floor, rushes past the reception area and shoots past Linda's desk.

"Excuse me," are the only words Cole hears before he slams the door to Sid's office. He paces back and forth, his hands grasping the sides of his head. Cole stops, turns and eyes Sid's chair, then looks at his Rolex. His rage seems to give him a view of the whole room all at once. All the objects start to shake. Then everything stops. An unholy silence envelops the room.

"Okay. . .Okay. . .I'm in control now. I'm in fucking control. Why destroy this office? The office didn't screw me. That bitch screwed me. No, she screwed that biker, and they're both are gonna pay; pay with their lives." Cole sits down at Sid's desk and reclines in the chair. He relaxes his arms and legs and lays his head back and rises up out of his body.

Cole approaches his home at a slow rate, allowing his anger to build as he nears. By the time he reaches the front door he is in a blind fury. He rises up and passes straight through the bedroom wall. Cole sees his wife lying naked on the bed, next to a man, but this man is different from the one he saw her with last night. "Who the Hell is this? Damn it bitch, how many cocks are you chuggin'?" The man's arms wrap her naked flesh, the flesh of his beloved Faith. As Cole watches them, his vision narrows to the point of blindness.

Cole eases back, then looks over at his chest of drawers and travels toward it. He reaches the top drawer and concentrates. It opens. He looks at his sheathed hunting knife amidst his socks and underwear. His vision narrows. The knife rises, and comes out of the sheath.

He turns his attention back toward the bed. The knife follows. The only thing he sees is his wife and her lover. His focus centers on his wife. As it narrows, he starts to feel the ivory handle of the knife. "Till death do us part." Cole's sight fixates on his wife's chest, then the knife plunges into it and twists back and forth. Faith cries a silent scream as her arms and legs spasm for a moment, then go motionless.

As Cole's vision widens, he notices the man's body stirring. Cole quickly narrows his vision to the ivory handled knife. The knife flies out of his wife's chest and streaks toward her lover's throat and stops. Cole looks at the steely blade of the knife pressed against the throat of his dead wife's lover's. Never did he want another man dead as much as he wanted this one, and in an instant he would be. "See you in Hell, you fuck!" Cole could feel the ivory handle of the knife as he slit the man's throat. He viewed the man's blood spurting out of his jugular, and thought back to his days at the CIA. "Why not a murder/suicide? The cops eat up that shit."

Cole focused his concentration again on the knife. "If this felt anymore real, I'd swear I was actually holding it," thought Cole as he moved the knife to the dead man's hand. As Cole's focus shifted from the knife to the corpse's hand, he felt an object on his little finger, a familiar object. "What the. . .Oh my God!" Cole looks down to recognize the pinky ring he received from the CIA on the dead man's hand. "It's me! I just killed myself! But, but how?!"

As Cole's vision widens, he recognizes his lifeless body lying next to that of his slain wife. "Wait, maybe this is just a dream. Think Cole, think. . ." Cole reflects on the events earlier that morning. "One minute I'm lying in bed, and then the next minute I'm taking a shower. But I don't remember getting out of bed and. . .that's it! I must have fallen asleep after fucking Faith and dreamt everything afterwards. I dreamt getting dressed and going to work. And when I dreamt I was projecting from Sid's office, I was really projecting from here. I went out, saw the Harley in the driveway, and came in and. . .Well, it's her fault. If she hadn't been. . ."

Cole is interrupted by voices coming from the hallway. The door to the bedroom opens and in walks Faith's younger sister Hope, a buxom thirty-four year-old brunette with green eyes.

"Sorry to wake you sis, but. . ." Hope screams hysterically at the sight before her; the sight of her dead sister and brother-in-law.

A tattooed long-haired Biker rushes into the bedroom. Hope turns and throws her arms around him, weeping into his chest.

"What the Hell is going on here? That's the guy Faith was humpin' last night; now he's with Hope. Can someone please tell me what the. . ."

"Didn't you get my note -- my note -- my note. . ." Faith's words echo through Cole's mind. Suddenly he remembers the folded piece of paper he used as a coaster the night before.

As Cole moves toward the door, he finds it difficult to focus and arduous to move. He feels increasingly weak, as if his life force is slowly pouring out. "Oh God, I'm losing myself..." He passes through Hope and goes out the door.

Cole drags what's left of his consciousness down the stairs and into the den. He makes his way to the cocktail table. His drink is still sitting upon the note Faith left for him. "Time's running out, got to focus. Please God let me focus; just this one last time." Cole hovers close to the note. He deeply concentrates, using every last drop of remaining energy to move the glass from atop the note. The glass slowly moves off, and the note unfolds.

Cole reads the note. "Hey lover. Do me a favor and don't go to our bedroom tonight. My weirdo sister and her grungy new boyfriend snuck up and claimed our bedroom, and made a mess out of the bed. After they left, she called and promised to make it up to us tomorrow. I didn't feel like washing our sheets tonight, so I fixed up a cozy little spot for us in the upstairs veranda -- remember, like in San Tropez last summer? I'm so lucky to have found you, my love. I'll show you how thankful I am when you come up here. My love forever, Faith. PS. Hope wanted to be there when you found out, but I want to share this with you alone - congratulations, you're going to be a Daddy!"

Cole grieves for what he had and what could have been as his soul slowly spirals towards oblivion.

From the Tear of a Stone
By Jenessa Gayheart

She opened her eyes as she awakened from dreamless slumber. Slowly, her sight roamed the rain-splashed scene before her to recognize where she stood, and all at once horror seared through her mind as she realized something had gone wrong. Terribly wrong. She shouldn't be seeing, or smelling, or even thinking! She stared in shock at the petrified arms reaching out from her body. They were not the flesh she should have seen, but rather a gray, crusty stone mottled with moss and decay.

She had turned to stone.

Stone cannot be alive, yet her eyes wandered the area through the wonder of being able to see, and the scene before her caused her every emotion to cringe. Yes, it was her home of Traepetti, except oh, how overgrown everything looked! Absently, she attempted to walk about, but in frustration realized how impossible that would be for her. She was just a human stone, but a frantically thinking one. She was alive! She knew this as she became aware of the distinct sound of splattering rain and watched as it fell in a thin curtain of wetness. Sadly, she could not feel it. She could only smell it and hear it. She was simply awake, not alive.

Carefully, her vision glided once again over the scene. What had happened to the village? How had it become so overgrown? So lonely? It appeared as though certainly more than even a year had passed since ... since what? She searched her sharpening memory, letting the tell-tale objects before her help piece things together: The stone body in the doorway over by the bath house; the one on the steps of the inn, and by the fountain; the many crumbled remains of what used to be whole human likenesses. She felt an emotional shiver as the horrible memory of the Monster Cluth returned. It may have happened a long time ago, yet suddenly to her, it felt like just yesterday.

The Cluth had come to the valley, to Traepetti, and had brought destruction along with it. Every living thing was turned to stone by the time the beast became disinterested with the little village, leaving its petrifying odor to roam the valley. As the terror of that day began seeping back, she closed her sight and experienced a mindful sob, as her body was no longer capable of such things. She wanted to move; to feel the rain falling solemnly over the lonely village, creating a rather sad pattering on what used to be the public baths and on the statues which stood around her.

The statues! They used to be people she had known! All were intact, and wore the bitterest expressions of disgust and terror on each of their faces. Over by the bath house, she could see old Tetia, the lady who had been in charge of the place, still clinging to the door frame for support since she had lost consciousness as all the others had. Lorna, the baker's wife, could be seen at the fountain, her water jug long-since dropped and broken as she had let go of it to collapse on the fountain's edge. The fountain no longer ran. Dark rainwater filled it now, and dry, brown leaves and dead twigs floated in the pool where Lorna's arm had slid down into the then-fresh drinking water. Just ahead, she could see Deros the blacksmith standing by himself, leaning on the iron banister of the inn where he had frequently drunk Hammeo's wine. His face was one of terrible disbelief.

She remembered more: Herself. She had been Panlia of Lethua and had come to Traepetti a year ago from the North where her family died when she was only fifteen. When her husband also died she had come to this valley with her four-year-old son, Julius, to look for a new life with her uncle, and had found it in the little town of Traepetti. She took to village life right away, and Julius adjusted to it wonderfully.

Julius! Her sight darted about, dread filling her at the thought of her treasured son having been turned to stone. Where had he been? Seeing someone's half-crumbled head at her feet, she frantically closed off her sight as the face began to look familiar. Her emotional heart beating rapidly, and with a mental sigh, she realized it was too big to have been Julius'.

Lying about the grassy stone yard were chunks of people who had fallen in the time since the tragedy, and had broken, having no hope of ever returning to normal. Was there any hope for life? Did she have any chance of being herself again? How long had it been? Did anyone escape? Maybe Julius did and that's why she can't find him. Had he grown up, or was he already dead? How long had it been!

Panlia stopped her frustrated thoughts. She forced herself to focus on where she was, which meant facing her loneliness. But maybe she wasn't alone. Maybe everyone who hasn't broken is still thinking like herself. She glanced around to see if she could tell. No, it was too hard to try through the curtain of rain. Besides, what would she look for? Stone people have no changing expression.

Becoming discouraged, Panlia stopped looking, and letting her mind wander, she remembered how it had all happened.

A sunny day in spring. Yes, she could remember that like it had been just the day before. She and Julius had gone to the weaver for a needle and fabric. And she was talking to Mesia, the seamstress, about the day and Tetia's new baby, letting Julius run to his friends at the town square's climbing tree. When the stench wafted in, everyone had assumed it was the cattle from out in the nearby field. But then it kept getting heavier, and choking. The air turned musty, and she remembered that Mesia even looked up at her in question. Nobody knew.

Then, Panlia remembered the horror on the seamstress' face as she grew slowly pale, then gray. Panlia could hear her friend's flesh crackle and stiffen, and as screams of realization pierced the air, Panlia began to feel her own skin tighten, and her blood run cold. She had rushed to the stone wall marking Mesia's shop, and beckoned to her child who had been climbing the tree next to the inn.

"Julius!" Panlia closed her sight as she remembered losing consciousness.

Recalling the awful day, she could feel the memory of her heart beating rapidly, and it seemed as though it had just happened. She had reached for Julius while leaning across the wall, her arms outstretched, and the child had been in the tree just across the way. She saw him crying, coughing wildly as he tried to call back to her, his curling fingers extended, turning gray, strangled with the awful magic of the Cluth's reeking odor. She herself had become stone before she could see her son turn completely lifeless.

And now, here she stood, leaning across the same wall which had through the years grown over with weeds and moss. She opened her sight, now knowing why her arms were outstretched, and with a hopeful spirit turned her eyes toward the tree where her child had been.

No one could be seen in the tree anymore.

Painfully, she let her gaze drop to the ground below. Her hope fell dead at the sight of a small stone arm, barely visible, what was left of its tiny fingers curled piteously. A crumbled stone body was hidden in the grass near the tree, missing its extension.

Panlia let her sight fog and then blacken as the tightness in her soul did its best to fill in the empty spot where her boy used to be. A tear made its way undetected down her rough stone cheek.

It finally stopped raining. A bird was singing nearby, helping Panlia meet her seventh day of awakening. During the passing days, she had experienced nearly every emotion she could through her many thoughts, the question of time passed since the Cluth being the most pressing. She guessed that it had been a significant length of time; more than a year, possibly more. But she couldn't be sure. The thought was constantly on her mind.

Panlia hadn't cried for anyone she had known specifically, save her son. She tried not to think about the pathetic lifelessness of the once-happy village. She wanted to concentrate on and grasp the present better. It was hard. She felt she would understand more easily if she could move her head around to survey the surroundings behind her; find another perspective.

Meanwhile, she was asking herself more and more questions. Another one had come to her that morning. Why hadn't anyone come into the valley from outside? Obviously no one had, or something would have been done – a memorial, signs of warning for other wanderers, even a burning of the village. Yet all stood there, untouched, unseen. Then it occurred to her: who would want to explore a village cursed by the Cluth? She sighed in despair that nobody cared enough to seek out Traepetti, now empty and forgotten. And she, the only inhabitant who could wonder these things, had to live there alone. If only for another soul!

That evening, after resting her eyes from the all-too-familiar sight in front of her, she surveyed the scene once more as she had over and over again, looking for something new to find. Usually, she would see a newly-grown flower or an animal straying into the dilapidated rubble of the fallen village. She just the day before realized that there was the next of a sky dart in the hollow of Lonia's skirt, and that the vines crawling along the ground from her wall turned dark-gold every evening.

But this day, she sensed a change rather than actually seeing it. Troubled at not being able to see what it was, she searched the square thoroughly. There was Tetia, still clinging to the door, and Lonia, yet lying at the fountain's edge, and Deros at the... Deros!

Panlia stared at the man, not yet knowing what it was that struck her about him. There was no new physical change, but a deeper one, a feeling in the air. Some sense of completion, of less hollowness in her senses, of added "being."

His face, she thought, look at his face! His expression had been frozen between disbelief and realization, yet now she also saw wonder and curiosity... and pain. It wasn't there before, she was sure of it! She wanted to believe he was there, somehow projecting his feelings so she could sense them, but she was afraid she might be imagining things due to her being so alone. Was Deros really awake? How could she know for sure?

"Deros, can you hear me?" she timidly tried thinking to him. She got a reaction. It felt like "Who's there?"

She didn't hear it. He couldn't have possibly spoken anything. Their world was made up only of emotions and senses, but she sensed a distant confusion, frustration, fear. Panlia could feel that it wasn't her own confusion, it was distant. She knew that it was from the man at the banister of the inn. A surging feeling of joy and lone-less-ness filled her, but it was quickly followed by a wave of pity for the man at the stairs. This man had just awakened to the bleak fate of their past. She felt she had to comfort him, and did the only thing she could.

He was looking around. She could perceive his observation, as though each other's sight had been turned into a common feeling. He caught the feeling as she kept her gaze intently on him, and felt her watching him. A connection was made.

"Panlia?"

It was an incredible feeling for one who had begun to lose hope. It wasn't a physical touch, but as close as either of them could come. She wanted to talk with him, but couldn't think anything to him clearly; she'd become so muddled with excitement. A touch! A mind with which to wonder!

"You're relieved," Deros spoke with the bewilderment of knowing what she's feeling.

"Yes!"

"You've been sad," He said. He was catching on quickly, communicating clearly. "Of course. It's a sad state to be in, but it's good to not be alone."

"No, I mean you've been weeping. I can see where the tears have been on your cheek. How long have you been awake?"

Tears? She hadn't known that tears were visible out of all of this stillness and stone. Is this the only sign of life the statues had to offer in wakefulness?

"This is my seventh day. It's been so lonely, and the thought of what's happened is hard to face. I didn't know I could cry."

"Is anyone else awake?" She had asked herself that question over and over since the first day. She hoped fervently that no one else was. Being awake as a stone statue tortures the mind and makes one wish there were a way out. How could a statue achieve death?

"No. No one else is awake," Panlia answered solemnly, "But we are," she emitted with gladness, to make the situation sound as positive as she could.

"I wish I weren't awake."

She had often wished that, too. In the ensuing silence, she felt Deros looking desperately about the town and countryside behind her. Oh, if only for a new scene! She couldn't get away from the view before her. Every time she opened her sight, she saw the same people, same buildings, same broken arm in the grass. Never should she have taken her stroll into town every morning for granted - the trees, flowers, cottages, her boy's soft hand in hers. But now, she only saw her crumbled friends and the broken arm. If she had another chance, she would take everything in! Every color, shape, change of scenery, even the sting of a bee would be appreciated. The longing filled her.

"What do you see, Deros?" She waited eagerly for his reply. He was her only other window.

His pain seared through their existence, and Panlia sympathized, but hungered to picture a new scene. A new sky; hills; houses. She knew what was behind her, but she wanted to see it! Deros seemed to take forever, and the pain he emitted grew almost to panic. Maybe she shouldn't have asked.

"I...I see Mesia," the man finally said with a forced, calming sigh, "or half of her, lying on the ground in front of what used to be her stand, right behind you. I see someone's broken leg in the tall grass…"

"Anything nice?" Panlia asked, hoping for some description of the trees or field she knew to be there, "Can you see anything beautiful?" The remaining roofs of a few houses, perhaps the temple down the hill…

"No."

Her speculation was cut short. Just "No"? There was something worth looking at, she was sure. She found beauty in the sparkling fountain water, flittering leaves, the sky dart's song. Why couldn't he try? He's forced into this situation anyway; he might as well see what good there is, as little as there may be.

But then, what could she expect his first day awake as a stone? With all he's known decayed and covered with signs of weakness and age, she wouldn't blame him. Could she have seen anything hopeful in the broken stones and horrible faces before her when she first awakened? She couldn't grasp the good the first day; she would just have to be patient, but help him as best she could.

"I see weeds as tall as corn," Deros continued, "I see what must have been a wagon, the skeleton of a beast that must have wandered in here, the festival tree lying on the ground, leaning against a boulder- oh," Panlia felt a twinge of weak laughter, "That boulder is Ardos. I remember I had just seen him across the way when... "

His pain seeped in again, and there was silence. What could she say? How could she help him to see hope in the scene before him? Panlia resigned her efforts to knowing that time would help her to help him.

The pain ebbed slowly. "How long has it been?" Deros' question filled her senses. "I don't know for sure. Many years, I think."

The air then slowly became void of feeling from the statue at the banister, and Panlia's compassion grew as she felt him finally surrender to the situation. Hopelessness sifted in like a thin mist, and Panlia gazed at its source across from her. Understanding came to her when she spotted a wet line making its way from his eye down his hard, saddened face.

Yes, they could cry.

At the sky dart's song, Panlia became aware of the morning. She emitted a smile at the bird on the edge of the fountain; caught and took in the cool breeze; felt the dew drying off of her arms in the warm sun...at least, that's how she imagined the morning would feel.

Neither she nor Deros had said anything during the night, and she let things be, waiting until he would want to speak. Gazing on him in pity, Panlia's memory went back to how she had felt when she'd awakened to this world alone, shocked at the state of things including herself. It seemed like it had been eighty rather than eight days ago. And now, she would have an opportunity to put to use what she had learned.

She didn't want Deros to go through what she'd had to alone. But how could she help him when he never told her how he felt? Deros obviously felt the pain of such a dreadful change; why did he not share it with her as any other troubled human would? Why so distant? She would ask him this day. Softening her concentrated stare on the statue, Panlia came out of her questions and took in Deros' figure through a whole new light. Thoughts filled her of how she wouldn't be alone in the world with Deros there, and how maybe, by some miracle, they could find some way to come alive. Then answers they had wanted to know since they awoke would become clear to them, and they would be together until they truly died.

She focused all her thoughts on the possible life before her and smiled wistfully at the visions she saw in her head: a new understanding of life, the appreciation of a simple touch given or received, being able to put her arms around Deros once it was all through. They will have gone through a lot together!

Deros still hadn't spoken. She looked at him, now feeling a little impatient, and stared at him willfully, trying to wake him.

"Deros," she said softly, "Deros, come see the morning," She didn't succeed. The sleepyhead. He can't escape this way, she thought, sooner or later he will have to wake up and face the truth all over again.

"Deros, wake up," she directed at him, "I'm waiting for you, hope is waiting for you."

She got no response. A mental sigh escaped her as she gazed about at the morning again, the sky dart perched now upon Lonia's shoulder, singing. Panlia was calmed, amused by it. She returned her sight upon Deros. He stood silently. There was something about him. His cheeks were barely streaked with drying tears from the night before. A doleful look in his manner caused a rise of compassion in Panlia once more, her senses reaching out to feel what he was.

She touched nothing. A wisp of hopelessness still hung, a suggestion of emotional weakness, an air of resigning, but that's all that was left.

Suddenly all she felt was shock; disbelief, yet a perfect understanding of what struck her that morning about Deros. His face no longer appeared curious or astonished or even terrible as it had before he had awakened. Now it simply looked...dead.

"No," she managed to choke out of her mess of feelings, "No, you didn't. It's not right; not fair!" Her piercing stare would have disturbed any conscious thing, stone or not. It was a last attempt to find him, to search for that one chance she had to touch humanity again. But when he couldn't be found, when she realized she had really lost him, she couldn't help but face that her dreams of a hopeful future had dissipated. Deros' blank face told all she needed to know about his reason for giving-in to death. There was nothing here for him, and now there was nothing for her. Yet here she bled, anguish, hope, any care she might have had left, and it wasn't enough to die. Completely drained, Panlia could do nothing but let her sorrow flow from her eyes. The time had come when she couldn't even appreciate the song of the sky dart.

Panlia felt her whole being lurch in the night when she startled awake as though by a nightmare. Her every sense was throbbing like a quickened heartbeat. Something was going to happen. The feeling sat in her like wet clay, and the more she tried to shake it, the more settled it became.

She peered around anxiously in the retreating moonlight, every object defined mystically by its silver lace. What could possibly happen? Panlia tried to calm herself, close her sight and sleep again, but found it impossible. With a little more frustration, she looked around, once again finding nothing. Then the feeling blew in like a breeze with the dawn, a feeling other than hers, a feeling of expectancy.

Was one of the other statues awake? Was Deros awake again? Was it a statue somewhere else in the village? Could it possibly be an animal? They are known to have a special knowing of things about to happen.

Loud chirping startled Panlia, and she quickly turned her sight to Lonia upon which sat the sky dart, singing its morning song. She stared at the bird in the shock of one who has just been surprised, then laughed to herself at the state her nerves were in, and watched it with relief and nervous humor. She always enjoyed the familiar song waking her every morning. Panlia noticed with wonder, however, that the bird usually didn't sing this early in the morning, or it would have woken her this early in days past.

Through her pondering, the feeling which had come with the sun invaded her, turning into an inflaming curiosity and awe; a sense of questing; fulfillment of a goal. She turned her sight toward the hidden, green-infested cobblestone street entering town from behind the bath house. Where was the feeling coming from? Who else could possibly be feeling something so strongly that she could sense it this powerfully? Her sight would not leave the street.

Then she caught a sound which caused her every sense to freeze and tingle. She had just heard a voice!

The sky dart became silent, and as Panlia wondered in disbelief, it flew off over the village. There the sound was again, only of a different tone. Unmistakably, they were deep-pitched sounds of the voices of human men! Her frozen senses became thawed as all the hope she had lost filled her and overflowed. How long had it been since she'd heard voices? The far-off words tripped along familiarly, though she could not understand their language, and the sources moved closer, though not yet seen. She waited for these humans to appear at the road upon which her eyes had already settled. The foreign thoughts were gladly felt. It was the one proof that she wasn't imagining things from prolonged loneliness.

She felt that their purpose was evident. They were here for the mystery, for witness of the legend…

" …For the satisfaction that nothing can be done to help," A man appeared around the bend of the road. He was a handsome man wearing the strange, though obvious signs of a great warrior. Panlia filled her sight with him.

"Demesus, what could we possibly do for people turned to stone?" Another man appeared at his side, also dressed for battle, but not as regally. The sight of both of them almost seemed too much for her. Someone has come! Someone has finally found Traepetti!

Upon seeing the town square, both men stopped. Panlia felt the air stiffen with horror and realization. She was filled with their shock as she found that these two hadn't been sure what to believe about the tales of Traepetti, and only now were finding it all true. Apparently, these were the first full statues the two had seen, and it struck them powerfully.

"Demesus, what if the Monster Cluth is around? I can still smell death here."

"Torius," The warrior moved from his stunned pause, "this happened a hundred years ago and a Cluth cannot live forever," The great warrior turned and saw Tetia in her doorway, then peered over at Lorna at the fountain. Striding over to her, he knelt before the collapsed figure, and Panlia experienced his perverse human nature to stare death in the face. He cringed, though not so anyone looking at him could notice.

"Yes," Panlia said, "it is a disaster, but we aren't all like that! I can think; I can feel your emotions; I'm awake!"

"There is death here, friend," Demesus stood, untouched by her thoughts, and faced his companion who was yet standing at the opening to the road. They gazed about at the four statues. Torius looked at her.

Panlia had been waiting impatiently for either of them to see her and notice that she was awake. Dizzy with the excitement of even being looked at, her thoughts went out longingly towards the men.

"Yes, over here! I am awake and I know you are here to free me from being a stone forever! Demesus, please help me! Help me to become one of you! "

But her thoughts went unnoticed. She concentrated on their words in case any seemed familiar, but to no avail. She tried to move again, knowing that it wouldn't work, but desperately hoping that their presence would make it happen.

"Torius," Demesus strolled around the yard of broken brick and stone, "no wonder no one has come to this place. Not only did the curse of the Cluth keep them away, but no one would have the heart to face the horror still contained in each of these faces. Even just this would be enough for anyone to want to stay away."

As he said this, his eyes passed over her unseeingly and instead rested on Deros across the way. The warrior's long strides covered ground quickly, and he ascended the stairs in curiosity, touching the cold, mossy stone of what had once been Deros. It had appeared to be the most gentle of touches, but the corrosion of the long-standing stone figure became apparent as, to her horror, Deros' body wavered, then, slowly, keeled to the ground in a terrible, hollow crash of old stone upon crumbled brick. She wanted to scream, to cry out at what the warrior had done, but instead she shivered inside and instantly felt relieved that Deros had died before he had broken.

Demesus stepped over the rubble unsympathetically, and moved in her direction. His gaze landed on her arms and followed their direction toward the tree. He found nothing there. His gaze settled on her face this time, and she felt the sadness he felt for her statue. Unexpectedly, that sadness turned to wonder and his gaze concentrated on her face even more.

Suddenly anxious, Panlia realized that this was her savior, but not to bring her back to life. He was here to let her go. A wave of calm overcame her, and with her sight closed, she waited for him to near.

His breathing could be heard right next to her ear, and she sighed within at the thought of finally leaving, of the freedom, and could now wonder where her spirit would go. She smiled to herself, and happiness overcame her as, for the first time since she awoke, she felt a touch! The smooth, young fingers of a warrior traced down her cheek where past tears had chosen their paths.

As her mind filled with light, and she dissipated with the morning breeze, the warrior caught his breath. His fingers traced back up towards her eye where one more tear had escaped, trickling down the stone cheek. His fingertip caught the drop, and he stared at it in awe. Putting it to his tongue, the man experienced a wave of tranquility, and then knew that it was possible to help a person of stone.

Love is a Seven-Letter Word Spelled "S-W-I-Z-Z-L-E"

By Daniel Kurland

There was reason to celebrate. I had just successfully sold a short story in twelve parts to "Dwell" magazine. The story is told from the perspective of a different piece of furniture in each part, as the events around a spill of Bordeau on a loveseat are chronicled. "Dwell," a home décor and furnishing publication, doesn't typically publish fiction. In fact, they never have. But my ever-useful agent, Lawrence Lawrence, not only swayed them on the matter, but they are also now in talks with me to adapt the story for a younger audience for their soon to be released, "Dwell Jr." magazine. This was well paying work, and if the stories garnered enough buzz, Lawrence thought it might become a good leverage tool for me.

So as Lawrence and I celebrated, bottles were popped, and drinks were made. While we were mixing our drinks, I noticed a container of swizzle sticks in my cabinet that were given to me at some gaudy affair that I had never used before. Those colored, translucent modeled pieces of plastic shaped like things to make you think you were drinking at a beach, and therefore more relaxed, and therefore living the perfect life. Sticks shaped like palm trees, and flamingos, and sailboats. I don't know why I grabbed them; Lawrence was yelling; music was playing; but I took them, and thought they might be fun. At the least I'd hear the clink-clink-clink of the ice cycloning around my tumbler glass. We sat down and Lawrence arbitrarily grabbed two sticks, a neon orange palm tree, and a neon blue mermaid, plopping the former into his drink, and the latter into mine. Lawrence began a conversation with me, but I didn't hear a word.

As soon as my eyes locked with that mermaid swizzle stick, I didn't hear a word.

To describe what was so bewitching with this swizzle stick, one must first describe what was so lackluster about the *other* swizzle sticks. The other designs weren't nearly as detailed or interesting. Crude shapes would account for wholes. The palm tree had no leaves distinguished. The flamingo had no demarcation line between his feathers and his legs, and the less said about the sailboat, the better. Perhaps most obviously, these sticks were not made with love. Probably rushed products to meet a quota and satiate a demand.

But the mermaid was an entirely different story.

As I held the swizzle stick in my hand, turning it all over and inspecting it as Lawrence droned on, I saw the intense detail chiseled into the mermaid's face, the scales on her tail, the little coy half-smile filling up her face. Even attention was given to the small of her back, showing she was arching herself outward. These were all little touches that did not have to be there; that were not exclusive to how a mermaid must look, but were there all the same.

The curls in her hair.
Her eyelashes.

Deep, deep thought was put into this product, and none of the rest. Then, as soon as I thought I had discovered all of the mermaid's secrets, I noticed that due to the crook of her hand, and how her body was positioned, the stick could also hang from the side of your drink when you were done with it. So you could look at it - all of it - rather than depriving yourself of missing anything while you enjoyed your beverage. None of these other sticks had this "second function." Most of these sticks barely fulfilled their primary function.

As days evolved into weeks, which evolved into months, I found myself using the mermaid swizzle stick in all of my drinks. Even ones that didn't need to be stirred. But there she'd be, hanging from the side, or hovering around inside, the half of her that's submerged, all distorted and stretched, but seeming to accentuate the stick's beautiful anomalies; magnifying them, as I watched the news or complained over the weather. It wasn't long before I found myself in bars, and the swizzle stick would be there. Bartenders would ask, "Where'd that come from?" but I wouldn't respond as I stared into the refracted plastic. I walked down the street as my hands would comb over the stick in my pocket, counting the scales on her plastic tail – 37 - tracing the ridges of her outstretched arm; resting my thumb in that detailed small of her back. And as I'd walk through the city, I wouldn't hear the traffic sounds, or see the "walk signs" flicker, I only felt the mermaid in my pocket. I was in that pocket too, and not on the street.

This was all fine with me, honestly. I didn't see it as a problem. Simply me trying to insert beauty into my beverage time, and really, is that despicable? Is that not what the inventor of the decanter or novelty ice trays was attempting? Besides, it wasn't affecting my social life. In fact, I had a date for the evening and all was well. And did that not entitle me to enjoy a cold drink with my favorite finned female while I waited? I couldn't think of a better way to spend my time...

The phone rang.

It rang and rang, and rang again, finally knocking me out of my stupor. It was dark now. The ice in my drink long melted; the hands on the clock long shifted. The phone rang a third time, and I answered it, never breaking eye contact with the mermaid the entire conversation. It was my date for the evening.

I had missed it.
Shrill yells bled from my receiver as I kept staring at the see-through blue inches before me.
I hung up the phone.
I re-filled my drink.
I stirred my stick.

I had been lost, staring at the swizzle mermaid for nine hours. The phone rang again. This time I didn't pick it up.

Saturday morning I poured myself a glass of orange juice, and began discussing my "Dwell Jr." alterations with my mermaid drink helper. Suddenly, it was Monday. The weekend, evaporated. I looked out the window. My eyes hurt. My stomach hurt. I hadn't eaten anything for two-and-a-half days. Now it was time to do something.

I felt like as with any great mystery or puzzle, one's natural fascination with it disintegrates once that puzzle is solved. So I thought that if I could track down the artist who designed the mermaid swizzle stick, I could ask them the inspiration behind it, study it, and put all of this behind me.

I had to.

I was not naïve enough to think that tracking down this person would be an easy task. Finding the company that made a random set of swizzle sticks made in Nineteen-Ninety-Anywhere, let alone the *person* responsible for this design would be likely be as difficult as finding an *actual* mermaid. As I examined the sticks though, it seemed that this journey would not be as difficult as I thought. The flamingos, palm trees, octopuses, and sailboats all had the logo MAMA'S FISH HOUSE stamped into their sides. A company that I could find absolutely nothing on and was surely long foreclosed when the swizzle stick industry didn't receive the boom that it expected. However, stamped on the mermaid sticks was something completely different. It simply said ZOO-SWIZ, and the copyright sign, and then the word Dallas. This was proof that this certain swizzle stick *was* made by someone else. Someone different who cared about what they were creating. And Dallas couldn't be a real hotbed for drink accessory companies. Had it said Los Angeles, or New York, or even Chicago, I'd have been concerned. But, Dallas? I could do Dallas. And having the name of the company and their location would hopefully be enough.

As I got up to begin searching for my answers, I could have sworn that the mermaid winked at me.

It took me a week. Which is an inflated amount of time, as I have to assume that every two hours I spent working was in fact thirty minutes of work, followed by being lost in the mermaid's intricacies for an hour and thirty minutes.

Or more.

But I came up with some answers.

To begin with, ZOO-SWIZ was closed, as I figured it would be. They were a small independent company, and by following the trails of the owners online, it seemed like Margaret Winslow Peckinpah was the artist that worked there during the 1992 to 1994 window that ZOO-SWIZ was operating.

Locating Margaret Winslow Peckinpah was a much more difficult task. The research I found seemed to indicate she was still in Dallas, but I couldn't find where. A regular person probably would have given up there. The makers of the palm trees, and the flamingos, and pretty much all of MAMA'S FISH HOUSE would have given up there. But not me. And thankfully, with the help of five-hundred dollars and Jimmy Turetti, a local private investigator, I had a phone number for Ms. Peckinpah. Now I just had to get her there.

It was a long elaborate ruse that led to Margaret Winslow Peckinpah flying from her Dallas bungalow to meet me in my New York City loft. A ruse supported by the purest of intentions. My plan was mostly just. Like a drink full of goodwill with ice cubes of deceit bobbing around the surface. And if you stir those ice cubes thoroughly enough, that deceit will melt and you'll just be left with a tall glass of altruism. I had told her that I was a reporter doing a feature on The Top 10 Most Niche Industries in Dallas in the 1992-1994 Time Period, and that I'd love to interview her about ZOO-SWIZ. I told her she came in third, right above the company in Dallas that made the plastic covers that go on the end of shoelaces, and just under the company that makes pewter Pearl Jam belt buckles.

My plan was simple enough. I'd have the mermaid swizzle stick out, in my drink when she came over, and I'd gage her reaction when she saw it, determining if she really was the one who designed it. Myself, Mr. Turetti, and the five hundred dollars I gave him were all fairly certain that this Margaret Winslow Peckinpah was the same Margaret Winslow Peckinpah that worked at ZOO-SWIZ. She had been incredibly brief on the phone, though, almost as if trying to avoid the subject, and while she did accept my invitation and plane ticket, and received the details of the interview, something still felt off. It was entirely possible that this was just some senile old woman who was looking for a free trip to New York City and the opportunity to blather on to a pair of wide-open ears. So I was satisfied that my "swizzle sting" would cut through the treacle and get me to the truth.

It was the day of the interview and I was spending far too much time orchestrating my far too simple plan. Every few minutes I was adjusting the placement of my drink on the table. Looking for where it would be the most obvious.

Where the light hit it best.
Where it was devoid of shadow.

Three hours later I determined that fifteen inches away from the width of the table, and seven away from the length was the perfect placement for it.

Then an hour later, I conceded that sixteen by nine was in fact more perfect. And it wasn't until I was trying to determine if the mermaid swizzle stick should be inside the glass, or hanging off the side, and which side to have it leaning on - war treaties were signed faster than this; obsessive compulsive disorder developed over less than this - that I heard a frail knock at my door that had to have been Ms. Peckinpah. I thought it was unusual that she was early. But she wasn't. It was when we had agreed to meet. I had just gotten lost in another Swizzle Circle; an event that was now so prevalent and expected in my life, I had given it a name.

When I opened the door for Margaret Winslow Peckinpah, I couldn't stifle the beaming smile that spread across my face.

She looked identical to the mermaid. The coy eyes, her hair; she even seemed to take my hand in the same way the mermaid swizzle stick clung to glassware. I felt like I didn't even need to continue with my experiment any further. This was obviously the artist, creating a monument of her youth and beauty, solidified in time in the form of bar-side accouterment.

We sat down together, me never breaking my gaze, afraid that doing so would shatter the whole illusion. I asked her pointless questions that provided answers I no longer cared about. She talked about plastic melting, and color dye, and pH levels, and Dallas legislation in the mid '90s, and all I could think about was just buying a one-way ticket to Dallas and living with this real-life siren. If I could be this committed to a swizzle stick, think how committed I could be to an actual person.

We kept flying through this interview that would never be printed.

Me jotting down fake notes.

My ears hearing Margaret talk about bureaucracy and my hands digesting it into sentence fragments like, "Margaret Winslow Zukko" and "Dallas = Mermaids = Everything." She never once mentioned the mermaid stick that adorned my drink. Even as my fingers strummed upon it as we spoke about the past. The interview was coming to an end, and while I was entirely content just knowing, deep inside, that this was the mermaid, and perhaps, like actual mermaids, she just wanted a quiet life of being left alone, I was still left unresolved. So, as I thanked her for her time, and she approached the door to leave, she said, "Goodbye" and I blurted out, "Is this you!" as I clenched the swizzle stick in my hand and rammed it out at her. And then Margaret Winslow Peckinpah burst into tears and fell to the ground.

She wasn't the artist, I learned.
She *was* the subject, but she wasn't the artist.
Her husband, Donald Dangulus Peckinpah, was.

The two of them happily lived together, living a modest life at ZOO-SWIZ, where they didn't have lofty goals other than making an enjoyable product, which they did, and honoring one another, which they did. Margaret was Donald's muse and model. They had bounced around unsuccessfully from job to job, Donald never being able to play the corporate games that they required him to; his work, passionless and dull as he often thought of his wife he missed at home. One day, he finally decided to combine the two. Make his wife the work and spread her beauty throughout the world. The world had seen enough palm trees, after all.

This reality was in fact more inspiring and touching than if Margaret had been the artist after all. This was not something fueled by vanity or the fear of tomorrow, but rather the dedication and endless love that a husband and wife can feel for each other. I excitedly asked Margaret where Donald was. How I could get in contact with him. That I'd even be willing to go back to Dallas with her and save him the trouble of - It was at that point that Margaret burst into tears again. Eventually, she gained enough composure to choke out the words, "Poor Donald's dead, honey. He took his own life years ago."

The saddest thing was that Margaret told me that Donald's suicide was because no one ever appreciated or cared about his work. He didn't have illusions that he was creating something greater than he was. He just wanted some sort of acknowledgment that people enjoyed what he was doing; that he should continue to do what he was doing, which it can only be imagined becomes all the more difficult when what you're creating is a monument to your wife. But sales steadied, then declined, then stopped entirely.

Flamingos were cheaper.
Sailboats were flashier.
Everyone loves an octopus.
And MAMA'S FISH HOUSE had twice the facilities, at half the price.

I just wish I had gone through my cabinet sooner; tried to contact Margaret faster. Surely these differences wouldn't have kept Donald alive, but who knows? The one thing I was sure of was that he had created something so beautiful and engrossing to me, it had devoured my days and taken residency in my life. I had spent nearly a thousand dollars trying to find out who was the gifted artist behind these plastic drink stirrers and the answer was a man, now dead, because he thought no one loved his art.

I didn't love his art either.
I was *in love* with his art.

And if I could have told him that, maybe Ms. Peckinpah wouldn't be returning to an empty bungalow in Dallas.

Margaret left, and I wanted to stop her, but I was too drained to say or do anything. We maintained contact, Margaret and I; it seemed like she needed a friend, and I was happy to be there for her. But our conversations eventually became less and less frequent, until we slowly drifted apart like people are wont to do, and they finally stopped entirely.

The second part of my new fifteen-piece story in "Dwell" came out today. This story was from the ottoman's perspective. I read through my piece in the publication, finally ending with the "For Margaret, my Mermaid" dedication that she would never read.

I poured myself a drink.
I stirred it with my finger.

Single Night

By Dorothy-Ann Grandberry

"Guys, I don't think this is a good idea," Hannah Coleman whimpered as she stood on the steps of the old Knox house. Her friends had decided earlier in the week this would be a test of bravery.

Stay a night in the creepy old house at the end of the street. Seemed easy enough.

As she passed, her sister patted her on the back. "Come on, sis!" she said cheerfully, "it'll be fun! What's the worst that can happen?" Reluctantly, Hannah followed her sister up the front steps. As she walked in, she felt any icy breeze spread over her entire body. "It's kinda cold in here," their friend Jason announced, "everyone bring your sleeping bags?" They nodded in response.

The entire group consisted of four people: Hannah, her sister Penelope, and their friends Jason and Max. It was Max who originally planned the trip that Wednesday morning. At the time, Hannah was sure they wouldn't go through with it, but by Thursday evening, she was certain the group had made up its mind. Penelope begged her to come with them, and eventually Hannah gave in, but as she stood in the living room, she considered turning around and racing out of the house.

For the first few hours, they wandered around and listened to music. There was very little to see upstairs, besides unused guests rooms and the master bedroom. They lingered in the bedroom for a while, looking through the items that were left behind. "Come on, this is wrong," Hannah whined, "we shouldn't be going in his stuff." Penelope laughed at her. "You knew better than anyone that he was a terrible person. Think of this as him getting what he deserves." Hannah still didn't feel right about it, and she didn't participate, but she didn't leave the room either.

The time passed quickly, and before they knew it, the sun was vanishing below the horizon. Jason's expression began changing. Rather than a look of curiosity, a smirk began to grow across his face; a smirk that screamed 'I know something you don't know'.

They regrouped in a sitting room that was connected off the living room. Each of them had brought bagged snacks from the convenience store. After they ate their food, Jason stood from the floor and cleared his throat. "Everyone, I have a surprise for you!" he proclaimed, reaching into his backpack. Waiting a few seconds for added effect, Jason suddenly whipped out an Ouija board from his bag.

Hannah felt her skin grow even colder than it had before. She pushed herself to the opposite end of the room, refusing to move, and started to break out in a cold sweat. Penelope glanced at her. "Just stay there. You don't have to participate." Hannah crawled forward and placed her hand on her sister's shoulder. "Please Penelope, I have a bad feeling about this," she begged, her voice audibly shaking. Her younger sister shook her off and turned to the board. Seeing that she couldn't sway her sibling, Hannah moved away once more. Bringing her knees to her chest, she buried her face and squeezed her eyes shut. Hannah listened as her friends and sister chanted, persuading any spirits that were nearby to show themselves.

"It's not working," Max said flatly, his voice thick with disappointment. "Well I don't know what else to do," Jason countered, picking up his flashlight off the floor. Hannah brought her head up, thinking there was no danger and that the group had failed.

Suddenly, the three nearby flashlights started flickering wildly. The one dim light that had been working in the corner of the room immediately went out. The door slammed shut, causing Penelope to scream in terror. Wind rushed through the open windows for a few seconds, then fell closed.

Then, everything stopped. Not one of them said a word. They only listened for something; anything.

'We should've run,' Hannah thought to herself. Had she been any more confident, she would've said, 'I told you so.'

But she didn't have confidence. Even the never-ending supply of self-assurance Jason seemed to normally possess had gone south, leaving him alone with only his darkest thoughts. None of them dared speak. Max tried to rationalize the whole thing in his head; tried to tell himself that it was only the wind that closed everything and that they were in no actual danger.

But he knew he was wrong.

Max had read about these kinds of things before. Never about how to use a Ouija board, but always about what happened afterwards. Grim stories about people who had gone missing and were never seen again; the thought of people being torn apart limb by limb plagued his mind.

Penelope's thoughts went straight to what her sister had said only seconds before they started playing. Hannah told her that she had a bad feeling, and she begged Penelope not to play. Perhaps they wouldn't be there if she had only listened to her older sister.

But no, Penelope hadn't listened. She was always envious of the things her sister had, and Penelope decided to make this the one thing that she couldn't. It selfishly made her incredibly happy when Hannah proclaimed that she wouldn't take part in any way. Finally, something that Penelope could say that she did on her own, out of her sister's shadow.

At that moment, they heard something. It was a music box. But rather than the gentle music they had heard as children, this song was distorted and garbled. Elsewhere in the house, there was another sound; the soft humming of a young child.

Eight ears listened as something came down the stairs they had explored only hours before. After the initial commotion, there was nothing. No sound; no movement. Just when Jason was about to speak, there was a rough scratching at the door. Penelope's body visibly shook. The sounds continued on, causing their skin to crawl. Finally, when the carving ended, they cautiously excited the room.

As they turned down the hall, they came upon a message scratched across the door. Deep in the paint was:

Let's play a game

Surrounding it were smaller messages, three of them, and all exactly the same.

Not it.

Out of nowhere, a shadowy hand swam across the floor swiftly and clutched Penelope's ankle. Penelope cried out and grabbed at anything she could; kicking and screaming as the invisible force dragged her out of the room and down a dark hallway.

Hannah was frozen in her place. Jason ran forward to help her, but was stopped. At first, Hannah couldn't see what caused Jason to be stilled, but as she tilted her head, she could see.

A young boy stood in front of Jason, his palm outstretched and signaling him to stop. Wispy blonde bangs covered the boy's eyes as he whispered through cracked lips, "She's playing the game." The kid repeated that phrase three times then turned and walked lazily down the hallway, his music, the music from the music box, playing the whole way. He disappeared into the shadows, and the second the song ended, spurts of blood shot out of the walls that covered Jason's face and clothing. His eyes were wide in fear, and his mouth gaping in a scream that had been lost in his throat as blood continued to spurt onto his face for several moments before finally subsiding.

He fell to his knees, his legs no longer able to support him. Max ran down the hall with his flashlight in hand. "You guys gotta see this!" he yelled back. Hesitantly Hannah joined him and immediately wished she had stayed as far away as possible.

Written across the wall in her sister's blood was:

How fun. Play again?

There was no body, just the note. And once again the words on it were scribbled underneath. Max read it off first, followed by Hannah. Suddenly, there was the sound of the music box. The duo turned around. Jason stood there, staring down at the young blonde child. The child reached out and offered his hand to Jason, who slowly extended his back.

"No!" Max shouted at the top of his lungs as he lunged forward to stop his best friend, but the same shadow that had dragged Penelope away not only held him at bay, but pushed him back and sent him crashing into the blood covered wall. Hannah was no expert, but she could easily tell by the sound of the impact that Max had broken at least one bone. She watched as Jason combined hands with the small child.

One minute, the kid was standing there, plain as day. The next, he'd dissolved away.

Jason blinked rapidly and looked down the hall as a lonely light on the ceiling flickered on. "Max!" he yelled, racing to his best friend's side. Max was in a great deal of pain, but cringed away from Jason's hand. "What is it?" Jason asked. Hannah took a small step closer to him, peering closely into his eyes. Something about them was off. They seemed…darker than normal.

A smile spread across Jason's face. He burst into a fit of maniacal laughter that no one could seem to stop. "Jason? Are you alright?" Hannah asked softly. His head fell forward, his bangs covering his face. One of his hands came forward and grabbed hers, his fingers like icicles, and fell back with a primal screeching.

Jason stood at the other end of the room, staring straight at Hannah's frightened figure. "Why didn't you want to play?" he asked, his voice slightly warped sounding, "do you not like my game?"

The light she'd been so thankful for earlier flickered on and off. Jason had been standing far away from her, but when the light would come on for that brief moment, it allowed her to see his fingers. They were burned badly, as though he dipped them in gasoline and then lit them on fire. Not wanting to die, she flung her hands forward and grabbed his face. Jason let loose another scream, this one deeper than the one before it, and fell backwards onto the ground. As quickly as they could, Hannah and Max stood and ran back into the sitting room, locking the door behind them.

"We can't keep running," Max exclaimed, "even if Jason, or whatever is inside Jason, can't move through that door, the shadow will." As if called on cue, the dark hand crept slowly underneath the door and twisted the rusted bolt, unlocking and opening it with ease. Frozen, Max and Hannah looked to the doorway. Jason stood there, covered in Penelope's blood.

Re-emerging, the shadow hand grabbed Jason's head and slammed it against the wall then tossed his body forward as if he was a rag doll. Max ran forward instinctively to check on his friend. With Max only steps away, Jason laughed once again and turned his head to look at Max, a huge gash running down his face from the doorframe.

Even the burns from Hannah's hands were barely visible with all the fresh blood pouring from his face.

Jason continued to laugh as the blood rushed from his body and out of his head, spilling on to the floor in large splashes. His body seemed to deflate as the blood continued to rush out, and as he lay a lifeless mass of skin and tissue on the floor, the laughter somehow continued.

Max sat down and sniffled. "It's going to be okay Max," Hannah soothed him as she stroked his hair, "we'll find a way out." He winced in pain, though, when she attempted to put her arm around his shoulder, and for a moment she thought that he too had been possessed by the child, until she remembered that he had been smacked against a wall only a few minutes before. "Here, let me take a look at that," she said.

His shoulder was broken; that much was obvious. "Can you move it?" she asked. He nodded and grimaced in an intense amount of pain as he lifted his arm about five inches into the air. She nodded and stopped him. "That's good. At least we know it isn't out of the socket."

Max lowered his arm back down to his side and sighed. "You know we aren't going to make it out of here, right?" he asked her as he sank to the ground in despair. Hannah sat beside him and tried her best to smile, even though she knew that the shadow could come back at any moment and take either one of them. "That's not the right attitude. If we think really hard about it, I'm sure we can think of a way out," she attempted to comfort him.

Scoffing, Max replied, "Big words coming from the girl who didn't even use the board." Suddenly, he hopped up from the ground. "That's it!" he exclaimed. From the ground, Hannah looked up at him. "What's it?" she asked, confused.

Getting down on one knee, he used his good hand and held one of hers. "You didn't use the board! Did you see the way

Jason screamed when you touched him? Maybe you're somehow immune to the demons," He sounded hopeful, and at that point, they were willing to try anything to protect themselves. "All we need is a way to test it," Max said as he thought hard about the situation.

As if called on cue, a figure stood in the doorway. It was the boy. His skin was seared across his face and his left arm. Across his face was a deep scowl. "Look what you did to me," he muttered, "I better call my mommy."

From the floor, the shadow rose up, slowly taking on the form of another person. This time, it was an older woman who reminded Hannah of her mother. The woman wore tattered clothing with duct tape across her mouth. In her hands was an axe. She swung the heavy metal head around in the air a few times, finally releasing it and sending it flying at Max, severing his injured arm.

Blood spurted from the wound as he collapsed to the ground in pain. Hannah fell beside Max, shielding him from the towering figure. Hannah watched as the woman stopped, looked at the boy, and shook her head. "What is the problem?!" the child demanded, his voice becoming hungry, almost ravenous, "Kill them! Make them an example to let everyone know that this is what happens when you enter our home without permission!"

Once more, the apparition shook her head. Hannah looked on and studied the situation. The woman threw the axe back, securing it in Max's other shoulder. He gasped as it cut through the bone.

He stared up at Hannah, his eyes pleading for help. "I'm sorry," she whispered, tears streaming down her face, "I wish there was something I could do to help you. Please, just hold out until morning." Moving her attention back to the mother and son, she saw the mother reach up and pull the duct tape off her mouth. Her jaw was open, revealing a mangled mess of flesh and tissue where her mouth should have been.

After a silent moment, the spirit let out a terrifying scream that even drove the boy away. "I'll come back to play later," he growled as he ran off and dissolved into the air.

The woman spun back around and glared at Hannah. Keeping her glassy white eyes on the young girl, she stuck the tape back over her mouth and quickly sank back into the ground.

Hannah snapped her attention back to Max, who was bleeding profusely. "In every article I read," he murmured, coughing, blood sputtering up from his mouth onto both of their faces, "there seems to be a theory to how to stop it all. You…need to find…the way." He was fading fast.

She knew for certain that there was no way she could handle the remainder of the night on her own. Hannah struggled initially, but the adrenaline allowed her to lift Max into her arms and carry him around the house. She was careful to peek into each room before entering.

There was nothing downstairs that could help them. The only place left to check were the bedrooms upstairs. Swallowing her fear, Hannah climbed the stairs one at a time, expecting something to come out of the wall at any moment and bludgeon her to death.

Finally she reached the top. For the insane terror she had felt on the way up, it was as though she climbed Mt. Everest. A horrible, cursed Mt. Everest stationed squarely in hell. "Start with the guest rooms," Max said weakly, "maybe there's something in there." Starting at one end of the hall she explored the entirety of each room, making sure to open every drawer and closet.

Every so often, she could hear the sounds of small feet patting along the floor. Every time she heard it, she would run to where she had sat Max down and hold her hands out, fully aware that it was her only way of fighting back. While she searched, she thought about her sister. Stolen so quickly like that. What would their mother say when she found out about what happened? Surely, she would not be happy when she found out that her daughters had been stupid enough to not only come into the creepiest house on the street, but to play with an Ouija board and summon a spirit that was trying to kill them.

Hannah clung to the hope that Max was right, and that maybe there were clues in the house that could lead to her finding an answer to why all of this was happening; and possibly a solution for it.

Nothing usable was in any of the guest rooms. That left only one room left in the whole house.

The master bedroom.

As she walked in, the first thing Hannah noticed was the large window that faced the street. From there, you could see into practically any house you wanted, and have a great vantage point in case anything were to happen outside.

She placed Max underneath the window, and as she turned to begin searching, she noticed that there was a particularly loud creaking sound when she stepped forward. Rolling her weight back, she rocked her foot across the spot. The increased creaking was startling. Max looked at her through tired eyes. "We need to check," he whispered. She bent down and dug her fingernails underneath the wooden floorboards. After a few attempts, she was able to get underneath the wood enough to lift a few planks.

Inside the hollow space in the floor were a dusty tripod, an expensive looking camera, and an orange envelope that had a little clasp at the top. Hannah was shocked to find that the camera still worked. The old man had to have died at least ten years ago, and with the amount of dust on the items, it was clear that no one had known about his secret compartment.

She flipped through the pictures in the camera. The first few were just pictures of the house when it was originally built. Hannah remembered that the house was only just being completed when she moved in, which was about twelve and a half years ago. Knox had lived there for the longest time, but because of a safety issue, a section of the house needed to be completely torn down.

"Let me see," Max said, trying to sit himself up higher. She held out the camera and showed him each of the pictures. Nothing in them really gave her any reason that was worthy of leaving his house haunted.

She opened the envelope. Inside were letters written by the old man and addressed to himself. "Take a look at this," she said, holding out the letters to him, "he was going senile. He wrote to himself every day to remind himself of what to do." As she reached one of the final letters, she screamed and dropped the piece of paper, ignoring it as if floated to the floor. "What's wrong?" Max asked, startled at her sudden noise. "Do you remember the little boy that used to live next door to me a few years ago, but then moved away suddenly?" she asked him, sitting herself next to his broken arm. He nodded and passed the letter to him, allowing him to gather the answer for himself.

She watched his face, knowing that when he got to the same part she did that it would surely change. She was right. When he saw that very sentence, his face grew pale. In the letter, the old man admitted to assaulting the little boy while the child was left in his care by his mother, and then attacking the mother. They were both blackmailed and left town as quickly as they could.

"Hang on," Max mumbled as he shook his head, "he had to be pretty old. I mean, he died of natural causes right?

There's no way a man as old as him would be able to attack and torture two people." "He overdosed on medication, but he was sick so they figured he forgot he took them and then took them over again," she countered, "you don't think…" Max stared at her, "that he killed himself?"

Hannah furrowed her brow. The new information wasn't going to help them much in destroying the ghosts, but she would most definitely help with a police file... that is, if she made it through the night to get it to them.

"Maybe its closure they need." She whispered, looking over at Max. His pale face grew even paler, if that was possible. Sweat beaded his brow, his eyes fighting to stay open. It took Hannah a moment, but finally it sunk in.

"No. No, no, no. Max! Max, stay with me, c'mon! I need your help, please!" The trickle of blood gushing from his arm had formed a pool, of which she was sitting in without even realizing it. She lept to her feet, startled by the amount of blood around her. The floorboards in the hall creaked. Hannah's head snapped up, her eyes searching frantically for the source.

"Ring around the rosie," Hannah felt tears welling up in her eyes.

"Max. Max listen. Did Jason tell you anything about the board? I need you to think hard." He took a raspy breath. "I don't know," he whispered.

"Pocket full of posies," Hannah suppressed a sob against the back of her hand in a vain attempt to keep the ghost child from finding them.

"Please," she whispered. "Think hard, please!" Max closed his eyes, racking his brain trying to find the answer. Suddenly, before his eyes, stood Jason. They were standing on the sidewalk of what looked to be Fifth street.

"Jason, you're an idiot."

"C'mon Max! It'll be fun!" He magnified the picture on his phone. "Get this, it says that if you happen across an evil spirit that you cannot channel back through the board and is 'roaming free in the world of the living'," His voice dropped a few tones and he wiggled his eyebrows in a joking matter. "Then all you must do is 'burn the board from whence it was released'." Max stared at him momentarily before scoffing, and starting forward again. "C'mon, quit being a Debbie Downer, it'll be fun!"

"Not if something happens!"

"Nothing will happen, it's just a superstition!"

"Like hell it is! You heard what they said, 'don't dabble in the business of ghosts'." Jason replied, however it sounded like he was underwater and Max's vision became blurry as well. When he opened his eyes Hannah knelt before him, eyes glassy with tears.

"Ashes," The ghost was singing.

"What do I do?" She whispered.

"Ashes," more singing. Max looked at her, then shifted his eyes to the door. There stood the old lady, the boy beside her.

"We all fall…" The boy looked at him. "down!" The old lady raised her axe. Hannah screamed. Just as the old lady was about to chop into Hannah's skull, Max dove forward, rolling the two of them out of the way.

"Burn it!" He roared, rising to her feet weakly. "I'll hold them off!" Hannah stared at him, a mask of sheer horror written on her face. "Go!"

Hannah made a mad dash for the door, slipping past both ghosts, of which neither were interested in her. The little boy giggled, starring at Max with a hollow gaze. The old lady grunted, readying her weapon. Max stood defiantly.

"Come at me you evil bitch."

And come at him she did. And right before Hannah's eyes, the woman decapitated him, and blood spurted everywhere, drenching Hannah's face and hair.

His final words were a whisper;

"Get the board."

The board was still in the sitting room. She needed to make her way back down the stairs and into the room, retrieve the board, and make it back up. There was no way to do that without running into the boy. And she knew that once she made contact with the board, she would be more susceptible to his attacks.

Creeping out of the room, she tip-toed across the wooden floor until she reached the bottom of the stairs. Taking them one at a time, she softly stepped to keep the boards from groaning beneath her weight.

"Where are you going?" a voice asked her from the top of the stairs. She looked up. There he stood, his arms at his sides and a teddy bear in his hands that dragged down onto the floor.

Close to the bottom story, she tried to race to the top. But the boy was faster, and with only a flick of his wrist, he sent her flying to the bottom. She landed roughly, clutching at her left arm.

'This was no time to lose focus,' she told herself. She staggered, but rose to her feet and ran into the sitting room. There, sitting nonchalantly in the middle, was the board, staring at her innocently as if it had done nothing wrong.

Hands shaking, Hannah picked up the board from the sitting room and ran towards the stairs. Bloody hand prints were scattered up the rail and the opposite wall. She started taking the steps two at a time. One the final one, her foot slipped through the board as it gave way, her right ankle twisting deeply inward. She screamed in pain, knowing that she had to have dislocated it. At least.

Crawling, Hannah pushed the board forward and used the strength in her arms to drag her body down the hallway that seemed to never end. Behind her, she could hear the familiar patter of little feet, letting her know that the little boy's spirit may soon be upon her.

"Please!" she yelled, knowing that even if he wasn't nearby, he could still hear her, "I'm trying to help you! Let me send you somewhere better!"

A hand grabbed her ankle, sending cold chills down her spine. She looked back. "I don't want to leave," the little child said quietly, " I want to play." Her body lifted into the air and then slammed back down. She could tell that her skin still burned the child, but he no longer seemed to care.

He just wanted her to die.

She remembered what Max had said, that once you interact with it in any way, he will feel threatened. Hannah was aware that the boy knew what she was trying to do, but she couldn't understand why he wouldn't let her help him leave the horrible place.

Hannah couldn't be sure of what happened when Knox was alive. What she fully understood was that Knox had spent years torturing the boy and his mother, blackmailing them for something hidden within the photos in his bedroom.

Lowering her body to the ground, the boy moved in front of her. He peered and looked over his shoulder at her destination. "You can't go in there," he whispered, "that's my playroom."

Tears began streaming down her face. "Why?" she demanded, "Why do you want to stay in a place so full of pain!?" He said nothing, and extended his hand to her face.

It was the end. She knew that at that moment that she was going to die, and that someone would come in the next day and see her body and all the blood scattered around. Or, perhaps they'd find nothing, and they'd forever be deemed as missing children. Hannah cursed herself for lying to her mother about where she was going that night.

She waited for his palm to cover her face; for any amount of pain to start. But no pain ever came to her. In her moment of terror, she shut her eyes tight. Slowly, Hannah opened her eyes and looked up.

An axe was buried deep within the boy's skull. He sat back on his backside with his head lowered, making sounds that one could mistake for crying. "Hello?" Hannah ventured. While she didn't want to have any contact with the child, he was in the middle of her path to the master bedroom, and he needed to move.

Without responding to her, the boy's head snapped up and he let out a deafening scream. She covered her ears and curled up into a ball. "Mother!" was all he screamed. Hannah snuck a look behind her. The mother figure stood there at the other end of the hall, blood covering her translucent frame. Seeing Hannah's gaze, the mother nodded at her.

Hannah pushed the board forward slightly and continued to crawl. The boy's attention seemed to be pulled toward his mother, confused as to why she had throw the weapon into his skull. Hannah did have to admit that her aim was impressive. The boy was smaller than her, even though Hannah was on her hands and knees. The woman would've had to have excellent aim to secure the axe in the exact middle of his head.

The world around her was growing colder. For a moment she thought that if the ghosts didn't kill her, hypothermia would. But, the doorway was in sight; her destination at hand. Suddenly, her broken ankle was yanked back slightly, and her face twisted in pain.

"I will not let you take me away! This is my playroom!" the boy yelled. His mother was doing what she could, but it seemed the boy's power was growing.

And he was calling in reinforcements.

More shadows monsters traveled along the ground and emerged from all corners of the room; Hannah could be certain that they were not her allies. They attempted to drag the board out of her grasp, but instead, dragged her slightly down the hall and back to her last position.

Feeling the adrenaline kick in, Hannah pushed herself forward even harder. She could feel fingers grasping at her clothes and neck, but she ignored the icy fingers and forged on.

Just a few steps farther.

She launched herself into the room, searching frantically for anything that could set fire to the board. Remembering the compartment in the floor, she began searching for any more hidden areas that could house a lighter or something similar.

There was nothing.

Feeling defeated, Hannah threw open the closet door and hid inside, even though she knew it wouldn't do much in the way of protecting her from the wrath of the child.

She could still hear his screams outside the room.

Unable to see in the cramped, dark space, she felt around until her hand met something square and familiar. Bringing the box closer to her face, she squinted until her eyes were able to adjust enough for her to see what was written across the label.

Matches, they were matches.

Why the old man had matches in his closet, she neither knew nor cared. She just praised the gods of coincidence and opened the box. Her hands were trembling, and as she opened it, the matches spilled all over the floor. She frantically searched for one and tried to pick it up, when the doors flew open.

The boy stood there, his body bloodied and gashed. Multiple shadows rose up on the walls behind him. "I'm tired of playing. It's time for you to take a nap!" he yelled, his voice growing deep and demonic. With the light streaming into the small area, she could see enough to grab a match.

Two shadows immediately dragged her out, as another two once again pulled on the board. "No!" Hannah screamed, striking the match on the ground and throwing it onto the board. The shadows let out painful shrieks and seemed to melt into the floor.

She turned and looked at the boy. His body was on fire; his burns matching the ones he received when he grabbed her skin. Directly behind his small form, the mother appeared, placing her hands on her son's shoulders, pushing him down into the floor and out of sight.

And like that, it was over.

Hannah watched as the board burned, the letters and numbers across the top becoming unreadable. It was amazing that whatever that plagued this house could cause so much destruction, and then be vanquished so easily.

She breathed a sigh of relief. Pain was enveloping her body, but at least she was going to survive. Hannah pushed herself up against the wall and stared out the window as the morning sun brushed over the horizon.

As she watched, she felt a cold presence enter the room. She turned around and saw the mother with her son in her arms, his sleeping head resting against her shoulder. Her mouth was no longer taped shut, and neither of their bodies were injured. Her son's face was not angrily scowling, but instead smiled happily as he could finally sleep in peace.

"Thank you for what you've done," the mother said, her voice soft and sweet. Hannah nodded as her breathing finally began to return to normal. The mother's expression grew sad as she went on, "I'm sorry, but you cannot tell anyone what you saw here." Hannah nodded once again. "Of course, I won't ever tell anyone."

Her eyes growing hooded, the mother frowned. "I'm afraid it's not that simple. If they come and take this house down or they violate it, my son's spirit will return. I need to be sure you won't tell anyone of what happened within these walls." The knowledge of what she was about to do hit Hannah, and Hannah shook her head wildly and attempted to scoot back even further. Her back was against the wall as she begged and pleaded. "Please don't do this to me! I'll never breathe a word of it to anyone!"

"That's right," the mother said, rhythmically nodding her head up and down, "you won't breathe. Ever again."

Gently, she woke her sleeping son and placed him on the ground. No toys were around, but he reached forward and pulled his music box out of thin air. Turning towards her, Hannah got a glimpse of his crystal blue eyes as he stood in place, twisting the small metal knob at the bottom of the box.

Opening the lid to allow the music to play, the boy began walking toward her. "Please no!" Hannah begged. The mother looked upon her sadly, "I'm sorry, but I need to be sure you'll keep our secret." Her son walked in front of her, stopping only inches from her face. He smiled at her, his blue eyes staring deep into hers. For a moment, she believed that maybe they weren't going to kill her. The song from his box ended, and his small hand crept up the lid and slowly lowered it, closing the box.

The last thing Hannah saw was the boy standing over her, his soft smile turning into razor sharp teeth, and then:

darkness.

Hannah's memory was hazy as she awoke in the hospital bed. "W-where am I?" she asked, unsure if there was even anyone around to hear her. Her mother realized she was awake and nearly killed her as she threw herself across her daughter. "You're awake!" she cried, "I was certain we were going to lose you!" Hannah grimaced in pain. Once Hannah had made it clear that her mother was causing her bodily pain, she stopped. Hannah asked her, "What happened?" She shook her head and responded, "You and your friends went to stay up in that old house…which I will punish you for later. Anyway, you got up to the first step, took one look through the doorway, and fainted."

She had fainted? But the blood and the death had all seemed so…real. Her sister's death was the worst of all, an image so violent she didn't think she'd ever be able to fully get out of her mind. As if on cue, Penelope walked into the room. "Hey. How're you feeling?" she asked. She sat on the edge of the bed and placed her hand on Hannah's arm. Hannah jumped at the contact.

Her hands were ice cold.

Author Contact Info and Bio:

Jason Peters – Editor/Author – <u>JasonAberrant@yahoo.com</u>

      Jason Peters is a Screenwriter, Author, and Founder/Editor-In-Chief of Aberrant Literature. Residing in Los Angeles, his works include the horror/comedy/crime-thriller screenplay *Obsidian*, and he is actively writing his first novel. Please contact via e-mail to discuss business opportunities, and follow on Twitter @JasonAberrant.

Rob Watson – Author - <u>freelance_storyteller@yahoo.com</u>

      Rob Watson is a horror/sci-fi fanatic and has been imagining and writing stories for as far back as he can remember. Some of his idols are Rod Serlling, Steven King, David Cronenberg, Edgar Allan Poe, Alfred Hitchcock, Wes Craven, and Dan Curtis. Rob studied film and creative writing at LBCC and CSULB, after which he spent several years working on movie production crews in various capacities. He has written almost a dozen feature-length screenplays, as well as numerous short stories and scripts. He has also recently started his own film production company, Damaged Psyche Productions.

Author Contact Info and Bio (cont.):

Jenessa Gayheart – Author - jenessagayheart@gmail.com

Born in 1974 in British Columbia, Canada, Jenessa Grimm Gayheart was raised with well-read parents, and grew to naturally appreciate the proper use of the English language. She wrote her first sci-fi/fantasy saga by hand in college-ruled notebooks, squandered job-hunting hours in front of a computer writing her second fantasy novel, and created dozens of short stories with magical twists along the way. In 2014, she self-published her third novel, The Story of Eidolon, and she is currently earning her AS degree with an emphasis on writing in Portland, OR.

Daniel Kurland – Author - danielkurland1@gmail.com

Daniel Kurland is a freelance writer, comedian, and critic, whose work can be read on Splitsider, Den of Geek, and across the Internet. He recently completed work on his noir anthology graphic novel, *Sylvia Plath's The Bell Noir: A Rag of Bizarre Noir and Hard Boiled Tales* and is the creator of the surrealist podcast, "Bic Zukko's Forever Almanac". His sketch troupe, Business Computer also performs a monthly show in Manhattan. Talk to him about bottle episodes of television on Twitter @DanielKurlansky.

Author Contact Info and Bio (cont.):

Dorothy-Ann Grandberry – Author - daskateonice@aol.com

Dorothy is 17 years of age, and is the author of the novel "Fallen", available at the world's largest online book retailer.

Jared Wojcik - Graphic Design - Jared.wojcik@gmail.com

Jared is a freelance Graphic Designer based out of Los Angeles, CA. He designed and created the Aberrant Literature logo, in addition to numerous other logos and design elements for prominent businesses, including Fortune 1000 companies. Please contact via e-mail to discuss design-related business opportunities.

There's plenty more Aberrant Literature to come…

Keep track of all of the newest stories at www.AberrantLiterature.com

Stay in touch with Aberrant Literature via:

Facebook: Aberrant Literature

Twitter: @AberrantLit

If you liked this Aberrant Literature Short Fiction Collection, please post a review at Amazon, and let your friends know about us. All honest and unbiased reviews are appreciated. Stay tuned for more collections to come!

www.ingramcontent.com/pod-product-compliance
Lightning Source LLC
Chambersburg PA
CBHW060641130626
46555CB00002B/906